The Candy Cane Cottage

The Candy Cane Cottage

JENNIFER GRIFFITH

ISBN: 9798367911237

This is a work of fiction. Names, characters, places and events are creations of the author's imagination or are used fictitiously. Any resemblance to actual persons, living or dead, events or locations is purely coincidental.

Cover art by Blue Water Books, 2022.

For Gary

Part I: Chapter 1

Jeremy

"You're going *where,* exactly?" Mark's voice crackled through the cell phone as I drove through the tree-lined two-lane road that led to Wilder River. "Never heard of it."

The curves on the winding, snow-lined road tugged at me with their laws of physics, and I kept my truck's speed a hair too fast for comfort. Just like old times.

"Nobody has. That's why I'm going." Not true. I had other reasons for going back to Wilder River. Make that *one* reason: Danica Denton.

"But, dude! Houston Properties just signed that deal acquiring the high rise at the crossroads of Georgetown and Prince, two hundred units, all majorly profitable."

I knew that. Everyone knew that. As my lawyer, who'd drawn up all the paperwork for all the contracts, Mark knew better than anyone. Why repeat it to me? "So?"

"So, dozens of clients are going to hear about it and come knocking on your door. We've got momentum. Houston Properties is set to be not just the top commercial real estate broker west of the Mississippi, but the top commercial real estate broker in the whole country—and you're going into the hinterlands? Now?"

"Yes." And for precisely the reason he mentioned. "I closed with

Georgetown." My eighteenth commercial property acquisition this year. "It's time."

Time to finally see Danica again, that was. *She can't blow me off now.* I'd been back to Wilder River a few times at the holidays, but I'd avoided seeing her, and most everyone else. Skipped the rumor mill.

Not that Wilder River people heard much, if anything, about real estate acquisitions coups in the city, no matter how huge. But had I done enough in the past dozen years to prove I wasn't the screw-up she accused me of being?

Only Danica could be the judge of that.

I was banking on her logical mind taking charge, accepting that time had passed and people could change, even persona non grata *Jeremy Houston*, the unmitigated knucklehead she'd claimed she would never forgive.

Never is a long time.

Today, I intended to prove that never was officially over. At least when it came to my chances with Danica.

The trees thinned from evergreens and gave way to blazing yellow and orange leaves, evidence of the shortening days. Christmas-like weather would hit Wilder River any day now, thanks to the elevation, no matter that the calendar still read October.

I slowed my truck as I approached the Wilder River perennial speed trap on the edge of town. Sure enough, an officer—probably Lonnie Parsons who graduated with us—sat behind his radar gun, aiming at me as I flew past.

Too late! Lonnie—or one of his compadres in blue—flipped on his siren and lights and whizzed out onto the road after me. I muttered a curse I'd learned in the military as I pulled to the side of the road, careful not to tip my truck into the barrow pit.

"License and registration," he said, not lifting his mirrored sunglasses as he stood at my window, where I'd pulled alongside the grassy ditch. "I clocked you at forty-nine in a thirty-five."

"I'm sorry, officer." I handed him my documents. "It won't happen

2

again."

"Jeremy?" The policeman lifted the tinted flap of his glasses and peered at me. "Jeremy Houston? Is that really you?" He reached into my truck and clamped his hand on my shoulder, shaking me hard enough to dislodge my fillings. "It's been ages!" He pointed at his badge. "Lonnie. Lonnie Parsons."

"Hey, Lonnie!" I shook his hand, then I cupped my jaw. No, it hadn't been dislocated by his shoulder-shake. "I heard you'd become a highway patrolman. Laughed, of course, when they told me."

"Well, now I can speed legally—got my Dodge Charger doing a hundred and fifteen on the straightaway chasing down a speeder last week. Didn't even break a sweat. Speeder had drugs on him, and so double the fun. Booked him and everything." He could have blown on his badge and shined it. "Good to see you, man. Where have you been? You just up and disappeared from Wilder River. Nobody heard of you again."

Uh-oh. That was not good to hear. Not if I planned to count on Danica being impressed with my improved reputation. "I'm living in Reedsville, running a business."

"I hope it's all above-board. Nothing shady."

Unless he considered the current inflation rates shady, resulting in several of my investments from just two years ago tripling in value. "It's all legal, my friend." I gave him a smile. "Go ahead and write me that ticket."

"Nah, you'd just have to pay a fine and watch your insurance rates go up. Promise me you'll take the speed limit seriously and I'll let you off with a verbal warning. *This time.*" His voice held menace for a moment, and then lines wrinkled at the sides of his eyes. "Why are you here? Did you hear about Danica and come right over? Word travels fast. No wonder you were speeding."

"Hear what about Danica?" My mind hopped like a deranged cricket. *Danica was getting married. Danica needed help. Danica was hurt.* "Is she all right?"

"They think she'll live."

Now my heart hopped like that deranged cricket on a hotplate. "Just a second. What? Tell me what's going on." As in immediately. It took all my willpower not to reach out and grab his shirt by the collar and shake him like he'd shaken me. "Lonnie. Is Danica hurt?"

"Calm down, dude. Man, you've got it bad for her—as bad as always." He gave a chuckle, and I made imaginary fists around his neck. "Man, I'll never forget when you tried doing that romantic balloon release for her while she was horseback riding with her dad. That was wild."

More like the horse had been wild. Spooked by the balloons, her dad's horse had plunged headlong down the hillside from the trail, nearly giving the guy a heart attack.

My mistake.

"Lonnie." Now my voice held menace, and he finally seemed to notice. "Explain."

"Oh, Danica fell off the uneven bars over at Candy Cane Cottage. You remember, her gymnastics shop? Anyway, she landed on her head, but the rest of her is fine."

But her head wasn't fine? My throat tightened to one of those coffee straw diameters. "What's wrong with her head?"

"Aw, it's temporary, whatever it is. Lexie"—that was his high school girlfriend, and apparently still in his life, maybe his wife now— "says the neurologist is sixty percent sure she'll regain all her memories. It's more *when* that'll happen that's in question."

Sixty percent sounded *in question.*

I pumped Lonnie for information and finally gleaned that three days ago Danica had fallen, hit her head hard, and had been out for a whole day. Then, when she woke up, she'd had no knowledge of anyone, past or present.

"She must be terrified."

"Aw, you know Danica. She gets through things. She should be out of the hospital in a few days. They're still watching her. Bad bump."

His radio crackled, and Lonnie saluted me. "See you around? I hope you'll stay in town a bit. We'll have a bonfire."

Danica's head was injured, and Lonnie was thinking about food? Typical Lonnie. He drove off in his souped-up Dodge Charger, and I fired up my truck and sped past Danica's rustic-cabin-turned-gymnastics-shop, Candy Cane Cottage, straight for the hospital.

Chapter 2

Good thing the flowers in these four bouquets from the hospital gift shop were already cut and therefore more-or-less on their way to dead. My grip on the stems would've strangled anything trying to stay alive.

At the information desk, I stopped to talk to Margie Fenway. "Danica Denton's room, please?" I shifted my weight multiple times while the volunteer in the sea green smock eyed me. "I'm an old friend."

She pulled her glasses down to the edge of her nose and peered over them at me. "You look like that Houston kid." Her lips thinned. "I was at Angelica's wedding. When *you know what* happened."

I didn't blink—on the outside. On the inside my eyes were squeezed shut in a horrified wince. So, my big moment lived on in the memories of the Wilder River populace. Twelve years! They should have done me the courtesy of forgetting, even if they couldn't forgive.

However sick I felt on the inside, externally I matched Margie, stare for stare—a tactic I'd learned in the army, and which had become my negotiating bread-and-butter in business. After a full thirty seconds, she relented.

"Danica is in room twenty-three. But if I hear that anything—and I mean *anything*—is wrong when you go to her room, you'll never set foot in this hospital again, even if you've been decapitated."

6

Wow. That was quite the image. "Thank you," was all I said and then swallowed hard as I made my way into the hospital proper. Whew. I'd passed the first test—of the dragon guard.

Unfortunately, the bigger test lay ahead. Every step, my feet grew heavier. This was it. I was seeing Danica for the first time in over a decade, and she might not even remember who I was.

This could go either way.

And I wasn't ready.

"Knock, knock." I rapped my knuckles on the frame of the open door. A curtain on rings hung to block the top half of the hospital bed. "Are you all right for visitors?"

The curtain whooshed back with a metallic swish. "Hi?" a feminine voice asked.

Danica! She looked the same as always but more beautiful. Her strawberry blonde hair curled in thick ringlets, and her soft blue eyes took me in.

My stomach and my heart and my throat all swapped places a few times. How could she have become even more stunning than she'd been when we were young? A swell of memory and love rushed up from the base of my soul, filling every cell of my body and spilling out in an overflow of emotion.

"Hi," I managed, but then had to clear my throat. The cellophane of the flowers crackled in my hand, like the electricity of longing crackling inside me. "How are you feeling?"

A white bandage wrapped from her forehead around her head, but her curls spilled out all around it. Her eyes raked over me with a questioning gaze. Her clear, pale skin was whiter than normal, or than I remembered, but that might be due to the hospital stay. Her rosebud of a mouth parted, and she spoke.

"Forgive me if I need an introduction." She touched her temple. "It's getting pretty old, having to be reintroduced to everyone I know and love. Even my mother had to tell me who she was, although she freaked out more when I couldn't remember my third great-

7

grandmother's name, so, please, don't take it personally."

See? This woman was every bit as wonderful as I'd built her up to be. So thoughtful—even of her enemy!

"No worries. I heard about what happened and came as soon as I could." I placed the flowers on the counter beneath the window—beside ten other bouquets. Not surprising. She was universally loved. "I'm Jeremy. Jeremy Houston."

I waited for the scowl to form, for her to press the *nurse* button and request security to escort me out. None of that happened.

At her blank look, I continued, "Jeremy Houston. We went to school together."

And I was the guy who chipped your tooth when I made you a batch of brownies and a piece of gravel ended up in it. The guy who left a standee of your favorite boy band's lead singer in the shower to surprise you but only ended up scaring the living daylights out of you when you saw it in the middle of the night. The guy who managed to foul up every single attempt to impress you. That guy.

"I was at your older sister's wedding." Might as well see if mentioning my final, most egregious offense triggered any big reaction.

Nope. None.

"My older sister Penelope and your older sister Angelica were best friends."

Nothing still.

I gave it one more shot. "You introduced me to Pepsi when we were kids?"

She slowly shook her head and lifted a shoulder in a shrug. "It's no use." She grimaced. "I'm basically at everyone's mercy. You say we're old friends, I have to trust you." A little smile formed—and then she looked me over, not with questioning, but assessing me.

After years of gauging competitors' reactions during commercial real estate brokerage deals, I'd gotten pretty good at reading nonverbal cues. To my shock, Danica Denton was appraising me and giving me full approval, right down to dilating pupils and touching her collarbone.

She was into me.

Danica Denton looked at me, the gnat on the windshield of her existence, and liked what she saw.

My knee buckled, and I tensed it to keep from toppling. Old friends. She's the one who'd used the term, not me. Add to that she'd been the one who'd always defined me as her enemy in the past. But … if she'd forgotten my wrongs, was I still officially her enemy?

I was here to right those wrongs, to clear up old feelings.

But if old feelings had evaporated with a bump on her head—did I need to bring them up now? She might regain her memories at some point and hate me all over again, or she might not. Through years of business experience, I'd learned to spot an opportunity for what it was. And this one was massive.

Again, I found myself shifting my weight—but this time, it was as if I straddled two paths, with a gulf between them.

Path A, tell Danica what she has really thought of me all my life and tell her I was here to apologize.

Path B, smile and play along. See where things go, play it all by ear, hope for the best.

"Old friends." I smiled. "Or new ones, if that's how we should define it." Absolutely, we should define it that way. I flashed her my best smile.

Danica blushed. *She blushed!* Then, she offered her hand. "Nice to meet you, Jeremy Houston, my new friend."

I took her hand, small but strong, and encased it in my own. Zings flew up my arm and pierced my heart. "I have a great feeling about this friendship." I grasped her hand a little longer, pressing it with what I hoped was meaning. "Let's just start fresh, if that's okay with you."

"It's our only option." She reclaimed her hand, but she placed it against the side of her face, which was decidedly no longer pale. "Thank you for the flowers. It's a lot of flowers."

Four bouquets, one for each time I'd totally humiliated myself while trying to impress her. Best laid plans and all that. But it didn't begin to cover the dozens of other times I'd only partially humiliated myself around Danica, the girl who'd stood up for me when I first moved to Wilder River. Thereafter, it seemed, I'd ticked her off every single time we interacted.

It killed me to think back.

But now—here was the opportunity. Golden, glinting in the sun. Danica *couldn't* think back on all those times. I really had been handed a clean slate and a fresh start with her.

"Sit down, please." Danica indicated a stiff vinyl club chair that looked easy to disinfect. "I haven't had much company today, and it turns out I hate TV."

"I know." I laughed. "You always hated TV. You said it was fake, and sometimes you wanted to reach inside and strangle the actors for whatever was going on."

Her eyes grew wide. "That describes my feelings exactly! What else do you know about me?"

What didn't I know? I'd been a student of Danica Denton for all my youth. "As a kid you loved riding your bike up steep hills just so you could coast down. You liked the wind to be fast to lift your hair, which you thought was too heavy for regular breezes."

She touched her hair. "It's really thick, isn't it? I bet it's hard to manage."

"You manage it beautifully." I looked at my lap. Human nature didn't respond well to fanboy behavior. I'd have to rein in my gushing compliments. Play it cool, as if this were a standard negotiation. "But you're right. It did get unruly."

She frowned. "What else?"

I made a list. She liked her grilled cheese sandwiches slightly charred; thank you notes—both given and received; that boy band from Australia, but only their second album. I hummed a few lines of their biggest hit.

"I remember that!" She joined in on the second half of the verse, singing pretty badly. "That's so weird. I can remember a stupid song about dancing on an upside-down cow trough, but I couldn't remember my own great-grandmother's name without help. Apparently it's my middle name." She sighed and fell back against her pillow. "It's discouraging."

"What do they say about your chances of remembering?"

"Fifty-fifty."

That low. Wow. I put up my emotion shields. "Do you know how the accident happened?"

She described her attempt at a leap between the uneven bars, and how she'd landed directly on top of her head. "Or so they tell me."

Oh, right. She couldn't remember anything. "Sounds painful."

She rubbed the side of her head. "At least they said no kids were watching at the time. It happened during off hours between classes. Did you know I'm a gymnastics instructor? Apparently, I own a gym called Candy Cane Cottage—which seems like a weird name for a gymnastics business, if I may say so—and teach a hundred kids tumbling and floor routines and balance beam every week." She shrugged. "Some of the kids came in and brought me pictures and cards they'd drawn for me." She frowned.

"I take it you didn't remember any of them by sight."

A line formed between her brows. "That was the worst, seeing their disappointment."

Clearly, they loved her, and yeah, they'd be disappointed to be forgotten. "I'm sure that was awful for you."

"Worse for them." She flopped back against her propped-up pillows. "I wish there were something I could do to speed my memory's return."

"Did the doctor have any suggestions?" The last thing I wanted was a speedy recovery of her hateful memories of me.

"Just rest, for now." She sighed as if she were the most bored person alive. "If only I'd cultivated a love of television. Then this place wouldn't seem like a prison."

Ouch. "Well, you do love to read."

"I do?" She brightened. "What kind of books?"

The air around me tingled. I knew this one. "Your favorite book of all time is *Jane Eyre* by Charlotte Brontë."

"Really? How do you know that?"

Because she'd thrown it at my head. "Would you like me to bring you a copy?"

For a second, she hesitated. "Yes, but ..." Obviously something bothered her. "But—and this is going to make me sound like even more of an invalid. Don't think of me that way, all right?"

I leaned forward and placed a hand on her shin, though it was covered by the hospital blanket. "Go on."

Danica glanced at my hand, where it lay on her leg. She didn't move her leg, but she did sit forward. "My vision has been incredibly blurry. I can't even read the paperwork they keep asking me to sign."

The hospital was insisting a woman with memory loss sign legal documents? My blood went from normal to boiling in an instant. "You can't read right now, and you're signing?" A hard edge crept into my voice. "Don't do that anymore, okay?"

"But they're in a hurry, and I'm sure it's nothing but boilerplate stuff, and—"

I held up a hand. "I've got a business partner who is an attorney. We're going to have him look at every single thing you've signed since you were admitted, and you're going to promise me right now that you'll take a photo of every paper they put in front of you and send it to him for verification before you put your name on anything."

The clock ticked in time with her blinks. "You're freakily serious."

"Contracts are important. Signatures matter. Don't get stuck, okay?"

Finally, she nodded. "You're really protective of me." Again, her cheeks pinked. "Just what were we to each other before all this?"

Ignoring the question, I pulled out my phone. "This is Mark's number. I'll tell him to watch for texts from you and to prioritize them. And when the nurse comes in next time, you ask her for copies of all paperwork in your file." I wrote down Mark's name and number. "She's going to balk and act like it's a lot of work, but hold her to it. She'll have to do it. I'll make sure Mark gets it, and we'll make sure everything is above board."

"This is Wilder River's hospital. Not some scary big-city asylum, you know," she said.

"And you're compromised." And I'd learned the hard way not to assume altruism in anyone. "Trust but verify. We're just verifying."

Danica let out a long, slow breath. "As much as this *watch out for your legal life* stuff should probably freak me out, I'm weirdly relieved to feel like someone is looking out for my best interest. It feels kind of foreign. Well, everything feels foreign, so it probably doesn't count." She smiled and laid a hand on my upper arm, since I was standing beside her now to place Mark's info on her rolling dinner tray. "You're a good friend, Jeremy. It's good to have a friend."

Friend! Yes!

Now, I realize that a lot of guys would define this as being friend-zoned. That being called *a good friend* by the one woman I'd crushed on since I was a kid might be termed a major defeat.

Not me.

Anything where she wasn't scowling at me and threatening to have me tossed out on my ear or any communication from her that didn't involve the phrase *pressing charges* was huge.

"Hold on." I pressed a few buttons on my phone, opening a retail app, finding what I needed, and hitting buy, and then download. "I have *Jane Eyre* on my e-reader app."

"Jeremy!" Danica's face broke into the smile that I loved, even if she always hated it because it showed too many teeth down the side. *Like a hungry wolf*, she'd lamented. "You did that? For me?"

"I only have time to read you one chapter."

"But I'll be left hanging."

"Well, let's say that I'll come back another time, if you text and ask me to." I placed the ball in her court. Not quite in the same way it'd

13

been in the past, but I had to think about these things, about the eventualities if she got her memory back. "Especially if you make the text really dramatic."

"Oh, I can do that." She grinned.

"Good. I'll put my number in your phone." I should've put Mark's, too, but a plan formulated, and I didn't.

She handed me her phone, and I added my name and number. When I handed it back, she frowned. "It's weird. If we're friends, how come we don't have each other's numbers?"

"Chapter one." I settled into a chair beside her bed and launched. "There was no possibility of taking a walk that day. We had been wandering indeed, in the leafless shrubbery an hour in the morning; but since dinner (Mrs. Reed, when there was no company, dined early) the cold winter wind had brought with it clouds so sombre ..."

Slowly, Danica settled back against her pillows and listened to the first chapter of the classic novel, with all its melodrama. I'd read it before. Guess why. It was pretty good, but mostly because Danica loved it so much.

By the time I got to the last paragraph of chapter one, she'd closed her eyes. A nurse came in and took her blood pressure, waking her up, and telling me that visiting hours were over for now. I could come back at seven if I wanted to.

"Jeremy, would you?"

"Text and tell me how you're feeling. I don't want to wear you out." She did look tired. I'd been in the army hospital a couple of times. Visitors were more taxing than most non-hospitalized people realized. "Have a good nap." I'd remind her about requesting her medical documents later, when she wasn't so tired.

Outside her room, I leaned against the tiled wall. Whew. That had not gone at all like I'd expected when I left Reedsville yesterday. A jolt ran through me, and I punched a fist into the air. Voices interrupted my victory dance.

"Who was *that?*" The young nurse's voice dripped jealousy. Ha.

"An old friend, I think." Danica gave a long sigh. "Jeremy Houston."

"Just like the weather in that town: hot, hot, Houston." The nurse sighed right back.

"Yeah. Totally. Erm, I mean, he's incredibly helpful."

"You like him."

"I hardly know him." A pause. "But based on what little I do know, he's seriously amazing." Danica giggled.

Actually giggled.

"I eavesdropped a couple of times." The nurse's voice asked, "Are you going to text him to come back?"

"Is the Pope Catholic?"

On that tired old metaphor's cue, I swaggered down the hallway and out to my truck. Four bouquets of flowers, an e-book, a lawyer on retainer, and a rip-roaring case of amnesia. Perfect recipe for getting Danica to not only forgive me, but to say I was *seriously amazing.*

The truck's engine roared to life, and so did an idea.

What if I can do more than simply get her to forgive me? What if she could fall for me?

Chapter 3

"Hey, Aunt June." I knocked on the screen door of the white clapboard house at the base of the Wilder River foothills. From here, the clearings of trees beneath the ski lifts made snakelike trails up the mountainside between the dark evergreens and blazing red maples. "How are you doing?"

Aunt June, seated in her recliner, pushed down the footrest with her legs and raced to greet me at the door. "Why, as I live and breathe!" She unlatched the little hook at the top of the screen and flung it wide. "Jeremy! It's been an age! Look at you, all grown up and manly." She threw her arms around me and dragged me into her house, seating me on the floral, faux-velvet sofa in autumn tones, shooing her big black cat off and picking up her knitting. "Get away, Scooter. That's where Jeremy needs to sit."

A game show blared on TV. Trivia. Aunt June muted it but didn't shut it off. "Tell me what brings you to town. I heard all about your Georgetown and Prince coup. You're hitting the big time, aren't you? Your parents are so proud. They told us all about it on the group text."

My mom and her siblings had a notoriously active messaging network. "It was a good week for business," was all I said. "And, to answer your question, I'm here to see about mending fences with an old friend."

My life must be an open book, because Aunt June frowned. "Sounds like you heard about Danica Denton's mishap."

"How did you—?"

"That accident was bound to happen. She's far too old to be flipping around on gymnastics bars!"

"She owns the gym, and besides. She's only twenty-nine."

"It's a dumb name for a gym. Candy Cane Cottage. What is that about?" Aunt June fussed and wadded up the forest-green yarn against the knitting needle in her hand. "Besides, *one year old* is too old to be flipping around on gymnastics bars. It's as if she forgot what happened to her sister." She flung the yarn in the air above her head, and it landed in her lap.

What about her sister? Danica's older sister Angelica had never been involved in gymnastics. Born with a leg so twisted, how could she have?

"Here's what I say." Aunt June pointed a finger at me, the partly finished Christmas stocking project flapping. "Some people can't seem to learn from other people's mistakes!"

"I can't even seem to learn from my own." I gave her my best grin, and she finally relented with one back. "Danica's a nice person. Her gymnastics students love her."

"Don't I know it? Everyone loves her. She's the nicest girl in all of Wilder River. Except when it comes to how she treats you. Which is why I could never forgive her." Aunt June folded her arms across her ample chest. "I'm your biggest fan, Jeremy. No matter what everyone else says."

Ah, there was the kicker. Everyone else in Wilder River thought of me as a disaster on steroids. And they'd been right. But for the past dozen years, I'd been proving them wrong. Not that anyone who wasn't on Mom's text group would know it. And not that anyone would believe Aunt June if she shouted it to the rafters in church.

Which was why my current course of action was a risk. At any point, someone in town could apprise Danica of my true reputation. Warped from reality though it was.

"She's a great person." I flinched as Scooter, the black cat, planted himself on my lap and began to shed generously. I liked Scooter, just not his chunks of detached fur. "Don't hold her too accountable. I admit I made some mistakes when it came to Danica."

"Scooter, get off Jeremy. Go outside and catch a mouse or something." Aunt June swatted the air five feet away from Scooter, accomplishing nothing. He started purring and hunkered down. I planned on lint-rolling for hours, later on. "Talk about mistakes! Your mistakes with Danica are legendary."

"I went to see her." I looked at my hands resting across Scooter's back. "In the hospital."

Aunt June's eyes bugged out. "And she didn't throw you out on your ear, threaten to have you incarcerated for harassment, call you inventive names?"

I shook my head, and a smile stretched across my mouth. "Nope. In fact, I think she kind of liked my visit." Kind of liked *me*. Thought I was *seriously amazing*. A warmth infused me. "I'd even bet she's going to forgive me." Or more.

"Bet?" Aunt June extended her arm to me, open handed, so far that her recliner nearly lost balance. "Put your money where your mouth is." There. That was the Aunt June I knew and loved.

"Fifty bucks says she lets go of her grudge permanently."

"Fifty bucks!" Her eyes narrowed. "Do you think I'm made of money?"

I narrowed my eyes right back. "Do you think you're going to lose?"

She slapped her hand into mine. "Let me think. What will I do with that fifty dollars while my favorite nephew writhes in embarrassment? I'll use it to pay for a grief therapy session."

"Grief therapy!" So many things happened in the family when I wasn't looking. "What have you got to grieve about?"

"Not me, you." She pointed a sharp knitting needle at me. "Danica is the nicest girl in town, but she's also the strongest-willed. Which is why you don't have a chance."

"Are you *sure* you're my biggest fan in all of Wilder River, Aunt June?"

A deep nod, and another fold of the arms over her chest.

Probably accurate, since no one else in this town thought even half so well of me as she did.

Except Memory-Loss Danica. Who thought of me as amazing. So there. I'd already cleared the first hurdle. "You'll see," I said. "Now, what kind of yard work or house projects do you need done this afternoon? Woodpile refilled? Christmas lights hung? I'm free until seven."

Because at seven, instinct told me I'd be getting a message from Danica Denton on the pretext of wanting to hear more of *Jane Eyre,* but really she'd be trying to get to know Jeremy Houston. I'd be glad to show her a little sliver of the *real* Jeremy Houston, the one no one else in this town had any clue existed.

Sure enough, at the town church tower's stroke of seven, a text chimed in my phone. I set down my hatchet in the back yard where I was splitting logs into firewood and stacking it in Aunt June's woodpile, in preparation against the cold months.

Jeremy, my nap left me both rested and bored. This is Danica, by the way.

She didn't ask me directly. I waited for the direct request. I had my reasons for that.

Hi, Danica. I went back to splitting logs. Even though my default settings told me to jump all over this text, I'd learned a few things in life—like paying a girl too much attention didn't go over as well as my sixteen-year-old self had thought. Aloofness for the win. Or, so I hoped.

Perspiration beaded on my forehead. The pile had shaped up nicely.

Aunt June leaned out the kitchen window. "That's much tidier than you used to stack it, Jeremy. Nicely done. Do you want some hot chocolate?"

"Got any Pepsi?" My mind was skipping everywhere. I hadn't had any caffeine since arriving in Wilder River seven hours ago.

"You know that stuff will rot your insides." Aunt June shut the window.

I took that as the end of the conversation, and instead of going for the cocoa, I took a big drink from the ice-cold water from the hose. My phone chimed a few texts. I did not look at them.

Inside the house, I sat down with Aunt June, who had poured me a mug of cocoa anyway. I sipped from the edge of the steaming mug. The liquid burned my tongue. "That's pretty bitter, for hot chocolate."

"I brewed it that way. The bitterer the better. I've taken to only adding a teaspoon of sugar to the pot. Plus, I wasn't born yesterday. You and sugar are a bad combo." She mimicked a sci-fi laser gun, pointing everywhere—ceiling, walls, floor. "Pew, pew, pew!"

Did she think I was still five years old? "Have you seen Garrett lately?"

My phone chimed another text. I resisted again.

"He gets off work at the plant at seven, should be home any minute. I told him you were here—and that you're staying in his room, so he should scrap any secret plans he may have to move home."

Garrett was the last person to move home. "They made him foreman, right?"

"Youngest ever. They call him a *plant prodigy*."

"A high honor."

She grinned like she knew it was inane. "Proud mama here."

Really, she should be. Garrett was top notch. Valedictorian, all-around athlete, never got a speeding ticket, never ran shirtless covered in blue paint across the football field during homecoming to get a certain girl's attention. Garrett. The guy I'd been compared to all my life. *Why can't Jeremy be more like Garrett?* They'd whispered, but I'd heard.

But I couldn't hate him. He was too cool to even be jealous of. Plus, there'd been that tragic episode when he'd moved off to college and gotten married—briefly. We didn't talk about it. No one really did.

It was almost as if he'd forgotten, or wanted to.

"You'd better look at your texts. They might be from your mother. I told her you were here and that you'd been to see Danica Denton."

My eyes involuntarily shut. I scratched the side of my nose, fighting to keep control. "You told her?" I said, opening my eyes. "And what did she say?"

"Check your texts, sonny boy, and see."

Nice. This was just the type of thing that happened when a person returned to Wilder River. The rumor mill ground my life like so much grist within moments of my arrival.

The front door banged open. Garrett strode in, came straight to me at the kitchen counter, and yanked me into a bear hug. "Dude! You're here! How long? We're going to have the best time!"

I did not check the texts.

Chapter 4

"You didn't answer me last night." Danica's rosebud of a mouth formed a pout, one that tugged at my heart and made me momentarily regret my choice to watch a recorded football game from over a decade ago with Garrett—night of the infamous blue paint incident and Garrett's most famous Hail Mary pass into the end zone. "Did I have the wrong phone number?"

I set my Big Gusher cup of Pepsi on the windowsill and reached into the stuffed-full brown paper grocery bag I'd brought with me. "Let's play a game."

"Are you going to tell me what happened last night?" She folded her arms over her chest. It had a totally different effect on me than when Aunt June did it. I forced my eyes to stay where they belonged and not on the little crease of flesh that formed above the V-neck of her hospital gown.

"The game is called *Do You Still?*" First, I pulled out a half-pint clamshell of fresh raspberries. "Here's how it works. I'll give you something from this bag, and you'll guess whether you like or hate them. For starters, do you still *blank* fresh raspberries?"

"Love!" She leaned forward and reached for them. "Mmm."

Yep. She still loved them. "That was a gimme. Almost everyone loves fresh raspberries. Let's move onto the trickier items." I pulled out milk chocolate and dark chocolate. From what I recalled, she had a strong preference for one over the other. Yes, I'd guessed it wrong in an unfortunate incident deep in our past. "Do you still *blank* milk chocolate?"

"Love?" She opened the tinfoil and gingerly placed it in her mouth. I stared at her lips as she chewed—probably too intensely. They were sweet and mesmerizing. I was their slave. "Mm," she said. "Love."

Wrong. She hated milk chocolate and loved dark chocolate. The higher the cacao percentage, the better. "Good job. Three points."

"Yay!" She clapped and leaned forward to peer into the sack. "What's next?"

I handed her another piece of chocolate, very different this time— an eighty-six percenter. Might as well be eating cocoa powder straight from the can. "Do you still *blank* extra-dark chocolate?"

Her nose crinkled. "Hate?" she asked tentatively. "It's really bitter, right?" She took it and placed it on her tongue, killing me by inches. Slowly, she chewed it, her nose staying bunched up. "It's definitely bitter. If I liked it before, something was seriously wrong with me. I'm never eating it again. Blech."

"Three more points!" Okay, so I lied. The stakes were pretty low, though, or so I justified. But these results were exactly the type of feedback I was looking for.

We cycled through the rest of the things I'd brought—including other sensory items. She still loved the Australian boy band. Predictable. She could still finish a couple of sentences in Spanish when I started them for her—she'd be fine in Mexico City if she needed to locate that library. "That's big," I said.

"Being able to say *me llamo Danica?*"

"To find out that some things that you memorized from years ago are still embedded in your subconscious."

She sighed, running a hand over her head's bandage. "It's driving me crazy. Deep-seated stuff is still there, but little else. I feel like a new baby sometimes. Except I can walk and feed myself. And do math."

I broke into a circus announcer voice. "The amazing Math-Problem-Solving Baby."

She sang a little fanfare and then looked at me like I was her best friend. "I guess you don't have to explain where you were last night. Besides, my friend Oliver showed up, and you and I wouldn't have had time to read *Jane Eyre* anyway."

Oliver? Oliver who? My hackles all rose. "Oliver likes to dominate the conversation?"

"Oliver likes to talk about driving his trucks in the sandbox and getting his handstand."

Oliver. One of her tumblers. My hackles slowly relaxed. "I'm glad you had some company. But you're right. He probably wouldn't have loved hearing about Jane's new job with Mr. Rochester."

"Mr. Rochester? I thought you gave me the spoiler that Jane likes someone named Sinjin."

"Come on. You've read that book a dozen times. Maybe twenty."

"And it will feel brand new to me this time, which is all the more exciting." She aimed a warning finger at me. "No more spoilers." Her mouth spread into a grin.

I broke open the book—on my app—and read the next chapter to her, glancing up now and then to see her reaction to the events in the story.

"Listening to this story feels like a favorite old blanket thrown over me, even though I can't seem to recall anything that happens in the plot."

I set the book down, and looked into her eyes. "You may not remember everything, Danica, but you're still yourself."

Without warning, her eyes welled with tears. She blinked, but none fell. With a hitch in her voice she said, "You have no idea how reassuring that is to hear."

My own breathing caught. I looked down at the book and resumed the read-aloud. We made it through chapters two and three. Danica made comments now and then, insights into the life of Jane. "She's so self-sacrificing. I really admire that quality."

"Well, then you admire yourself."

"Me?"

I nodded, but before I could elaborate, they brought in her lunch. Then, doctors swarmed in, so I made for the exit.

"Jeremy? When are you coming back?"

"The next time you ask me."

"But last night—"

I left, toting my now-empty paper bag, which had proved to me exactly what I'd been hoping: that Danica could let go of old hates and change her mind. Not only that, she'd asserted her new opinions could be permanent.

If she could love milk chocolate, maybe she could change her mind permanently about me.

Chapter 5

Danica's text came early the next morning. I'd just put my credit card in the reader to buy my morning Pepsi. It'd taken the bulk of the afternoon yesterday to find a gas station that offered pellet ice, but it was worth the effort. No Pepsi experience is complete without the joy of soft-frozen pellet ice.

Can you come? I've got paperwork here, and I can't see well enough to read Mark's number on the note you left.

The Styrofoam cup crushed in my hand as I gripped it in hardly veiled triumph. I didn't respond by text. Instead, I called Mark.

"You're going to be getting a few documents from me in the next hour. Medical contracts."

"Dude. Are you all right? You didn't do anything crazy in Wilder River, like go mountain boarding and break your neck, did you?"

Mountain boarding at Wilder River Resort sounded great, but, "Not yet. The paperwork's not for me, but it'll still need to be kept confidential. I'll pay you for all work. Double if you do it fast."

"You already pay me double my hourly rate." But he agreed. "Who is this for? Not—not a *woman*."

I hung up and climbed into my truck, heading toward the hospital. Funny, I'd penned those numbers for Mark's phone pretty large.

Which could only mean *Danica wanted me there*. Saying she couldn't read Mark's number was just an excuse.

I tapped my fingers on the steering wheel to the beat of an inaudible rendition of "Let it Snow," the Christmas make-out song, which indicated my hopes that Danica might kiss me before Christmas.

Goals ought to have deadlines, right?

"Hey, what's up?" I strolled into Danica's room, bringing a container of homemade macaroni and cheese from last night's dinner at Aunt June's house that I'd saved for her, as well as my Pepsi. "Paperwork?"

Would seeing the Pepsi jog her memory?

"They are insisting I sign it, and you're right. I have no idea what I've been signing." She pushed a pile of papers across her rolling table toward me. "Last night, they brought me this old stack, plus more papers."

"You remembered to ask."

She nodded, her frown grim. "You don't think anyone's trying to pull a fast one, do you? I'm not at the top of my game. I'd be an easy target."

"We'll have Mark look them over. He's expecting them." I started snapping photos and sending them to Mark's email address. "Now, why did you really want me to come over here? Because it's not about the paperwork." I raised a brow. "Oh, here's something Aunt June made last night."

Danica accepted the plastic container and peeked beneath the lid. She took a deep whiff and then whipped it off. "Homemade mac and cheese? Seriously?" Without waiting for a spoon, she picked out an elbow-shaped piece and popped it in her mouth. "Mmm. I am in heaven right now."

Our eyes met, when she opened them after her pasta-ecstasy. "You're a good friend." Her voice came low, and macaroni-laden. Luxuriant. The voice I'd barely dared to hope would come from Danica to me. "A really good friend."

I'd love to be more than that. I came back with the most nonchalant "mm-hmm" I could muster and took the stack of paperwork off her makeshift desk. "How much longer do you have in here?"

"Those are my release papers. They're letting me go after lunch."

She was going home? Where was home? And who'd be taking her there? The room showed no signs her parents had been by to help, and they certainly hadn't monitored what she'd been signing.

"That's good. Are you feeling ready for that?"

"I'm feeling ready to get out of here."

Not the same thing. "Do you want a ride somewhere?" I had no idea where she lived. Presumably, neither did she. "Is someone else coming for you?"

"I haven't asked anyone yet." She worried her lower lip. "If you wouldn't mind …"

Little leprechauns performed a *Riverdance* exhibition in my chest. "Sure. Let me just check something." I thumbed through her paperwork and eventually found an address. "You live near the upper bridge."

"Probably." She shrugged. "I'm kind of a disaster."

A gorgeous one. "Until then, do you want to find out more about Jane Eyre? Will she end up with Sinjin, or is a dark stranger in her future? Dun-dun-dun!"

"No spoilers!" she cried. Then, she settled back and let me read to her again. We got to the part in the story where Jane began her service as governess at Thornfield Hall, when Danica chimed in again. "I think Jane really loved the children. Even though I don't remember much about my life, I have this sense that I always wanted to have children."

"You're a great coach, in the meantime."

"You know this about me?"

"Look at the evidence." I pointed at all the cards drawn by her tumblers. "And for the record, I always thought you'd make a great mom."

She gave a long sigh. "It's weird to not know and be stuck wondering why I never found that marriage and motherhood path." She gave me a pointed look. "Any chance you'd enlighten me as to why not?"

Because I'm your best match and you couldn't see me? "You'll figure it out."

Danica's look pierced me to the very center.

I resumed reading.

Not long after, Mark contacted me with a message. *Everything looks above board except this.* He'd drawn a red circle around a provision. *They're asking her to hold them blameless if a medical condition worsens due to negligence. I'll prepare a document for this by tomorrow.*

"What did he say?" Danica craned her neck to see Mark's message. "What's wrong? I can tell by the look on your face something isn't right."

"Mark will handle it."

"Whoever he is, it's nice to have Mark on my side." She wasn't speaking about Mark. She was looking at me. Man, this was working out a million times better than I could ever have imagined. "What do you do for a living, Jeremy?"

Before I could answer, a doctor came in and began the process of making final assessments before discharging her. I mentioned that the hospital would be hearing from Danica's lawyer about a mistake in the paperwork. Dr. Holden's eyes narrowed. "Is there a problem?"

"Just an oversight, I'm sure. Easy to iron out." I waved it away, but Holden suddenly became more solicitous of Danica's comfort. "Let's line up a wheelchair for your trip to the car. You're her husband, I presume?"

"No. But I'm her ride home." My response shouldn't have disappointed me as much as it did. *Someday I'll say yes to that.* "I'll bring the car around front, you bring her to the curb."

And Holden did. Personally. "Thanks for choosing us, Miss Denton, for your care." He shot me a nervous look. "You're Jeremy Houston."

"I am."

He looked at his phone, as if to check the time. "Houston

Properties. Commercial real estate broker."

I gave a solitary nod. He'd recognized me. He'd heard of my company. Which I assumed meant he would assume the business came with high-powered lawyers like Mark. "I'm sure between us, we can correct any documentation oversights."

"Yes." He cleared his throat. "The administration will be anxious to get any errors straightened out." He skedaddled.

My truck wasn't a lifted version, but it also wasn't built for a woman barely five feet tall. I held the door open for her.

"Is there a handle or something?" She looked a little helpless. "I swear, I really am a gymnastics instructor. Or so they tell me—so I should be able to make this leap."

"Alley-oop." Although I hadn't planned on acting like her knight in blue denim, I took both sides of her waist and hoisted her aboard. Then, I took the seat belt and reached it across her torso and latched it, my arm resting against her hip.

Danica's eyes met mine. A connection snap-crackle-popped like rice cereal in its first contact with milk. Her face flexed, as if swallowing back some huge emotion.

"All safe now," I said.

She nodded, keeping our gazes locked. "Yeah. Safe."

I shut the door and parked the wheelchair just inside the sliding doors. Then, I climbed into the driver's seat and headed out. "Do you want to go home, or would you rather go by the gym? Classes for the pre-school kids are in the mornings, so the school kids would be now, right?"

"How do you know that?"

"Honestly, it's just a guess." For once, I told the whole truth. "It's okay if you're feeling more like heading home."

"No!" She touched my arm. "Going to the gym might help jog my memory."

I rerouted, even though doing so might jeopardize everything I'd accomplished so far.

Danica watched out the window, taking in the shops and buildings of Wilder River. The Sleigh Bells Chalet motel, the vestigial local newspaper office, the bank, the hot cocoa shop. From atop Main Street, the ski resort presided over the town.

"It's quaint," she said.

"It's your home."

She looked at me and nodded. "Yeah, I feel that."

"Good." I didn't look at her. If I had, my heart might have exploded. She was so lost, so beautiful, and needed someone so much. If she'd known, she wouldn't have wanted that person to be me.

We arrived at her gym, Candy Cane Cottage. It fit her middle name, Candy. Did everyone know that connection, or just me?

I helped her down from the truck, and we stood on the ground beside it. I might have been standing closer to her than was necessary. Her floral scent wafted through my senses.

"The kids are going to be freaked out by this thing wrapped around my head. It's like I'm transitioning into being a mummy, starting at the top. Help me take it off?"

"Is it too soon for that?"

"They said I could remove it tonight anyway." She patted around, as if feeling for the end of the bandage.

I stepped forward and took her hand. Slowly, I guided her fingertips to the fabric's edge.

She looked up at me and breathed a soft, "Thanks."

That sole whispered word brushed through me like a feathery storm. Lifted me. Lightened me. "Uh-huh."

It took some doing, but she finally unwrapped her forehead. With a gentle caress, she touched what looked like a tender area. Yowch. I hid a wince.

"What color is it?"

"You've seen a plum, right?"

"Red plum or black plum?"

How like Danica to ask that question. "The last one."

Her face fell. "It will freak them out."

It might. "One sec." I went back to the driver's side and reached behind the seat. I came back to her with a truly worn baseball cap. "Wanna try it?"

She planted it on her head, sweat-stained brim and all. Her hair's curls sproinged out in all directions from it, and if I hadn't been well and fully smitten with her in the past, this image of her would have killed all hope of ever falling for another woman.

"You're staring. Does it look ridiculous?"

I cleared my throat and gave a nominal shake of my head. If I'd answered, I would've told her she was a goddess and possibly fallen at her feet in pure worship. "Let's go inside."

She took a quick look at herself in the side view mirror of the truck. "Oh, my hair's a mess." But she followed me toward the door. "This is a mistake, Jeremy. The kids are going to feel bad when they expect me to remember them, and none of them will look familiar. I can't remember a single name."

"Oliver. You remember Oliver, right?" Now, I prayed Oliver's class time was between four and four thirty p.m. "You can start with one, and go from there."

With a little gulp, she nodded and gripped my elbow. "You're right."

"I often am. More than you realize."

"What does that mean? Did we fight at some point, or something?"

"Or something." I held the door of the red-painted rustic cabin for her, and she went inside the candy-themed interior of the gym—red-and-white striped walls, pink polka dots, very festive and kid-centric.

My real-estate mind made a quick assessment: approximately six thousand square feet, high ceiling with exposed wooden rafters, a pair of restrooms, and what appeared to be locker rooms to one side. Simple, functional, and not a bad commercial property.

Immediately upon our entry, a petite brunette with close-cropped hair dashed toward us. She slammed into Danica with an intense hug.

"You're out! Oh, Danica! I am so glad to see you."

"Hi?" Danica looked to me, pleading for a save. "This is Jeremy. He gave me a ride, since I'm not cleared to drive for a while. And other reasons."

I recognized her. "Good to see you again, Tennille." Tennille Underwood, former cheerleader, slightly angry in the past. Very angry now.

Tennille's eyes turned to slits. "Jeremy?"

"Danica, this is Tennille, our old friend." Probably one of the moms of a tumbler by this time. My money said she and her beer-swilling jerk of a high school boyfriend, Liam, had gotten married and started a family. "Tennille, Danica is going to need *lots* of help relearning names."

"What are you doing here?" she demanded through clenched teeth. "What are you doing with Danica?"

Danica, fortunately, had been besieged by small, yelling, happy, loving children and didn't hear our exchange or catch the venom in Tennille's voice.

"You guys are so cute!" She hugged each one. Their moms soon took over, protecting her from too-enthusiastic greetings.

Meanwhile, a few steps off, I opened my palms upward, pleading, "She's not doing great, Tennille. Give her a break."

"Jeremy, you should *not* be here. What is this, some kind of opportunistic swoop-in, where you're taking advantage of her at her worst moment? Please. I can see right through this. Give me thirty seconds, and I will have all the dirt on you, and I'll be sharing it with her via my phone screen. You'd better get out of here, or I'm doing that right now."

What was to stop her from doing it if I left? I wasn't born yesterday.

"You're not going to do that, Tennille. Danica's in a fragile state. If you're a friend, you're going to let her heal before you hit her with a barrage of negativity. I've got a couple of weeks off work"—not true, but it would be as of the moment I messaged Mark—"and as far as I can tell, no one else is available to help Danica with the things she needs." Her parents never had been available for Danica. "Are *you* up to the task of fighting against the hospital lawyers over the fast one they tried to pull on her while her mental capacities were down?" When Tennille's eyes widened and then her face fell, I continued, "I didn't think so. But I am. And I'm on her side. I've always been on her side."

Tennille let out a snort to rival that of a gorilla's. "You. On her side!" More snorts. Not very ladylike. What would the cheer captain think? "It's more like you've been trying to sink her life to the bottom of the ocean. Every time you ever came near her, her life got exponentially worse, or have you forgotten? You're her worst nightmare, Jeremy Houston. And as her business partner, I'm not going to stand by and let you infiltrate her life with your—"

The rant was cut short when Danica came over. "They remember me, but I need Tennille's help with their names." She gave Tennille the most helpless, piteous look I'd ever seen. Even Tennille was thawed, although she gave me a final stern glance as she left me behind.

In what universe had Danica become business partners with Tennille Underwood? Geez. She'd hated Tennille in high school, hated everything Tennille stood for.

She hated you, too, dude, a voice in my head pointed out.

And then, I saw the opportunity in it: if Danica had forgiven Tennille for past transgressions, she might forgive me. Nice. I grinned, but turned aside so Tennille couldn't see my expression of triumph.

The gym smelled like chalk and sweat and air freshener. With a touch of swamp cooler for atmosphere. This place could really use a full-on air conditioning system, not that many places used them in Wilder River, ski resort town. But, with a lot of little sweaty kids, it could get hot. I made a mental note or two as I looked around.

"I can't believe this. Candy Cane Cottage supposedly belongs to me," Danica said, coming to my side as one of the coaches called all the kids back to the mats, "but it might as well be a foreign country."

"No sparks of recognition?"

She shook her head. "They're going to have a welcome back party for me next week."

"Yeah, well, ask them to postpone unless you're feeling up to it."

"I don't want to disappoint them."

There she went again, caring about everyone else's feelings. "You won't. Let's go."

Before I could leave, Tennille snagged me, and another mom raced to hug and talk to Danica. Under her breath, Tennille issued a stern warning: "Take her home. Then, stay the freak away from her. Do you hear me?" She drew a line across her neck.

Great.

Chapter 6

Needless to say, I ignored Tennille's threat. Instead, I made sure Danica went through the drive-through pharmacy, arrived home and got settled, had all her medications laid out, and waited while she showered. "I need to make sure you don't get a dizzy spell and fall down."

"I haven't been dizzy." She tilted her head at me. "But that's probably a good idea."

While she cleaned up, I did once again what every good real estate professional does: I assessed the property. Eighteen hundred square feet, approximately. Three bedrooms, two full baths, a living room and a large eat-in kitchen. The yard looked close to a third of an acre, but it backed up to the woods, and the property line might include a lot of trees. Drying autumn grass extended everywhere, with little oases of marigold-filled flowerbeds and even a gazebo with wrought-iron furniture.

It was everything I would've pictured Danica having in her life—minus the husband and kids. The place looked ready-made for a family. *I could help her out with that.*

The sun had set, and twilight blanketed the place, chilling the wood-smoke-filled air. So peaceful, I almost wished I lived in Wilder River instead of the city.

"Knock-knock," someone called through the screen door at the back of the house. "Whose truck is out front? Danica? Are you home?"

Uh-oh. That voice was unmistakable: sweet, but I'd seen the sour edge of it a few times in my day.

Her mom's voice.

My first instinct was to hide. Geez. I hadn't hidden from anyone since I was a kid, but the idea of confronting Mrs. Denton before I'd reconciled with Danica tore me to a million pieces. Bumped by my fingers, the straw squeaked in the lid of my Pepsi cup, and I cringed. For sure, she'd heard that.

"Danica? Are you in there?" The doorknob rattled, but I'd locked it. "Honey? I called the hospital and they said you'd been released into the care of a friend. We got back from our Norway trip as fast as we could, booking a flight the minute we heard about the accident." Well, that explained their absence. "Sweetheart? Are you in there? You're not answering your phone. I'm getting concerned. Whose truck is that?"

Too much had been said now for me to emerge from the shadows of the darkening house and come up to the door and respond. Like the coward I was, I waited.

Finally, after a few more pleas, her car's engine sputtered to life, and gravel crunched as Nancy Denton drove away.

Whew. I collapsed onto the sofa. Just then, Danica emerged from her bedroom, her fair hair damp but still curly, and her cheeks shiny from a fresh scrub.

A queen.

"I didn't faint."

Maybe not, but I almost did, drinking in her beauty. "Should we see whether you have any food in the house, or whether I should order you some delivery?"

A faint wince crossed her face. "Man, I don't know why, but the thought of delivery bothers me."

"All right, then. Let's check out the pantry."

The pantry ... was bleak. "Danica, forgive me for pointing this out, but when a woman's sole pantry item is Top Ramen, there's a

37

problem."

"Maybe I don't cook."

Then, my memory returned. She *didn't* cook. Big time. She'd failed culinary class twice due to multiple fires she'd set, and finally Mrs. Milligan had asked Danica to transfer to wood shop. "Now that you mention it, I should do the cooking."

Instead of the pantry, I checked the refrigerator. Good, good, good. "This will do." I pulled out a loaf of sliced bread, some cheddar cheese, and a stick of butter. "Prepare yourself to be dazzled."

It took me a few minutes, but I whipped up a couple of grilled cheese sandwiches. Mine, I cooked golden brown, but just as I was about to pull Danica's off the flame, a memory flashed up, and I left it on until a slight char formed.

"Voilà." I slipped it onto a plate, which I set in front of her, and then cut it in half on the diagonal. "Would you like steak sauce with that?"

"Do I like steak sauce on grilled cheese?" she asked, her eyes wide. "Let me taste it first. Why did you purposely burn mine, when yours is—"

I lifted a triangle's point and stuffed it into her mouth. She chomped down on it. "Mm." She talked through the crispy chewing. "It's really good."

"Do you still *blank* slightly burned grilled cheese?"

"Love," she muttered and then took another bite. "No steak sauce required."

For myself, I poured a tiny puddle of A-1 onto my plate and dipped a triangle point into it, the One True Way to enjoy grilled cheese. Albeit, golden brown. But who was I to question Danica's taste?

"Why do I get the feeling my preference is for burned grilled cheese because I burned it every time?"

"Not a bad guess. Maybe your memories are coming back." I took another bite, finishing my first half sandwich. "Or you always burned it because you liked it that way. Which came first, the burn or the preference for burn?"

Her eyes twinkled, and she took a huge bite. "Thanks for taking all this time for me, Jeremy. Don't you have a job?"

"I do."

"How can you take this much time off?"

"I'm the boss."

"But doesn't that mean you have *more* responsibility, not less?"

It did, but Mark was handling it. We were between major deals. I'd put off the Palisades Group, the Yellow Submarine Properties request, and the New Reach Real Estate people, telling them I'd contact them soon. They had all agreed to wait to hear from me. Mark didn't like it, but I'd just made Mark a very rich man, so he didn't have a lot of room to complain.

"Don't worry about it. When it's time for me to go back to work, I will."

Finally, she nodded, as if allowing me to keep some things to myself. "Let's have dinner together again tomorrow."

Chapter 7

The next afternoon, I took Danica for a ride into the hills above Wilder River. "You always loved the fall colors," I told her. "Though most are at higher elevations for now."

"Do you live in Wilder River?"

"Nope."

"Does that mean you'll be gone before the trees lose their leaves?"

"Not sure." I helped her into the truck. She wore a burgundy-colored sweater that hugged her gymnast body in all the right ways. *I'd like to be that sweater.* She caught me looking and didn't blush. Instead, she lifted a welcoming eyebrow.

I tuned the music to a playlist I'd prepared—full of that Australian boy band, plus a few classics that everyone our age knew by heart, thanks to their being overplayed on the local radio station when we were in junior high.

"Turn it up so I can sing louder." Before I could reach for it, Danica adjusted the knob and then sang at the top of her lungs as we sailed up the winding road into the higher elevations. Lonnie wouldn't pull me over again. Especially not if he saw Danica in my truck. Danica started laughing when I accidentally took a curve too fast. "You're making my stomach do flips."

She was doing the same thing to me with her hair flying swinging to the beat and her complete lack of inhibition while she sang. It was like this amnesia thing had peeled back the layers of reticence and fear, and all that remained was Core Danica.

I never would have guessed I could have fallen for her beyond the bottom of the deep abyss of *in love with Danica Denton*. But there I lay on my back, at the bottom of the world, staring up at the expanse of possibility.

Eventually, she turned down the radio and told me about her mom's visit, later on last night, after I'd left. "She wanted to know whose truck had been at my house."

"Did you tell her?" My hands froze on the steering wheel.

"It was one of a whole barrage of questions, so I didn't end up telling her about you. I hope you don't mind. It's not like I'm embarrassed by you. But I wanted to let you know it had come up, and it got sidestepped. Not on purpose."

"It's fine. I love your mom." Even if she didn't love me. "She's very protective of you and your sister."

"Mom said my sister is coming to town to visit and check on me soon. Did you know Angelica well?"

"My older sister Penelope was friends with her, like I told you, but I'm pretty sure Angelica thought of me as a nuisance."

"All girls probably think of their friends' younger brothers as nuisances." Danica brushed off my approximation of the truth.

Soon, we reached the snow-dusted summit overlooking the Wilder River Valley. I pulled over, parking the truck at an angle so we could look at the incredible view.

"Wow. It's breathtaking. With the sunlight hitting it like that, the river looks like a silver ribbon winding through fields of brown and gold." She let out a huge sigh. "It's strange. I feel like I've never seen it before and like I've seen it ten thousand times."

I stared at her instead of at the valley. She was God's most beautiful creation in this scene, as far as I was concerned. When she turned to me, though, I wiped the besotted look off my face and pulled my figurative rolled-out tongue back into my mouth. "Yeah. Gorgeous." My gaze reverted to the harvested fields and colorful mountainside.

"Do you wish we'd brought something to eat?" Nearby was a rest area with picnic tables. "I should have thought of that. I might burn grilled cheese, but I'm pretty sure I could figure out ham sandwiches."

From behind her seat, I pulled out a thermal bag. "Your wish." I plopped it in her lap.

"Lunch? A picnic lunch?"

In it, I'd included every single item I could ever recall her having in her lunch sack when we were in high school. Everything from Little Debbie Cakes, to those tiny tangerines, to string cheese to peanut butter on celery decorated with raisins.

"Yes!" She hopped out of the truck and raced over to the picnic table and pulled out the stuff I'd put together, one by one, with me arriving halfway through the extraction process. "I don't know why, but every single one of these things feels nostalgic. Which is weird, since I have nothing concrete in my memory to attach to them. But thank you." She looked up and met my gaze. "You're pretty amazing."

We ate, and then we stood awhile, gazing out over the valley. The wind whipped up, chilly—a hint of the winter's approach. Danica stepped closer, leaning against my arm. I wrapped it around her, and she nestled beneath it, where she fit perfectly. In a moment, she rested her head against my chest. It felt righter than anything right I'd ever felt.

And wronger. At the same time.

"Are you ever going to tell me about your life?" she asked after taking in the view of the blue and green valley's expanse.

"What do you want to know?"

"You're a boss, you said. What's your business?"

"I buy and sell property."

"I bet you're good at it."

I was. Very good. "It's been a learning experience."

"Have you always done that?"

"No. Only for about seven years. I spent time before that on active duty, and then I joined the Army Reserve. It lets me don the uniform a weekend a month and still run my business."

"I bet you look incredible in a uniform," she said, and then clamped a hand over her mouth. Through it, a nervous giggle escaped.

"You think so?" Heat flooded me. She was into me. And not just because I was nice and protective. Danica was attracted to me. "Well, you probably look great in your work outfit, too." I should *not* be picturing her in a leotard and tights right now. But she's the one who'd brought it up.

"Jeremy!" She swatted my chest, and then she left her hand resting there, pressing her palm against my pectoral muscle.

I didn't budge. Frankly, the longer she kept it there, the more my life expectancy would extend. We stood, touching, staring at the view— while I saw nothing but the picture of Danica and me together forever in my mind's eye—for some unknown amount of time.

Eventually, she spoke. "Military service. Your own business. Successful, I gather. Highly, or Mark wouldn't be at your beck and call. Why, Jeremy Houston, has some woman not snagged you before now?"

Wouldn't I love to tell her? "It's complicated."

"You've been married and divorced? That kind of complicated?"

"Nope." I'd better nip that assumption in the bud. "More like I have been waiting for the right woman." *You.* "Remember that game, hot and cold?"

"Surprisingly, yes." She half-laughed. "Of all things to be able to recall."

"Well, I feel like lately I've gone from glacial temperatures at the edge of the Kuiper Belt to the heat at the core of the earth."

"Kuiper Belt. That's where the solar system ends." Delight lit her features. "I'm remembering stuff." Dimples sank in her cheeks, and it was time to go.

She didn't comment on my *heat at the core of the earth* admission, but she sneaked looks at me on the way home. Gratified, and hopeful glances.

I needed to come clean and tell her the truth. Soon.

Chapter 8

"You're still chasing Danica Denton." Garrett slurped from his thermos during a quick break between sessions of putting up Aunt June's Christmas lights, which would be far easier before the snowfall hit her roof. "If ever in all history a guy had One-itis, it's you."

"What's that supposed to mean?" We leaned against the clapboard of the side of the house, the sunny side.

"You've heard of One-itis. When a guy gets so locked in on *one* girl that he can't see anyone else is alive. They overdo attention, and it's pathetic. Girls never fall for it. You're an alpha male nowadays, but she'll never see you for who you are unless you get over that."

I wasn't over it. Danica was the One.

Yeah, I'd dated a lot over the years, but I kept comparing every woman to Danica.

But despite the facts of my past failures with her, Danica was definitely starting to see me in a different light, judging from her texts. "I've got it handled."

"You haven't told her the truth yet, have you?" Garrett sipped until he slurped. "Come on, dude. If you don't, someone else will. Someone vile, like Tennille."

My skin crawled at the mention of Tennille. "Tennille already threatened to, but she hasn't yet. And Danica as she is now doesn't remember Tennille. She's spending a lot of time with me, and not really anyone else, from what I can tell."

Garrett punched me in the upper arm, making the pebble ice in my Styrofoam Pepsi cup rattle. "You dog." He chuckled. "But seriously, her mom is going to know. Be reasonable. The revelation is going to be better if it comes from you."

My cousin wasn't wrong. Fine, Garrett was *never* wrong. It was one of the things everyone worshiped about him. "I'll figure out a way. Soon."

"Good." Garrett set down his thermos and picked up another strand of lights. "Let's talk through it."

"You're pressuring me." I followed him up the ladder with another strand and some hooks. We got started again.

"Pressure turns coal into diamonds, Jeremy."

I stopped twisting the hook into the eaves. "Haven't you ever heard the phrase forgive and forget?"

"Of course."

"Well, I was in the living room with your mom on Sunday morning, and this televangelist had something very insightful to say about that principle."

"Lay it on me."

"Sometimes, we can get around the edict to forgive if we forget. Because if we totally forget, who cares? In essence, it's the same as forgiving." I whipped out my phone and looked up the text from the New Testament just to prove it to him.

"You, Jeremy Houston, are quoting Jesus to me." He wiped his brow. "The world certainly does change in unexpected ways." He attempted to stretch the strand farther, but lost his balance and had to pause. "But you still have to tell her. Because who knows how long her forgetfulness will last. And then what?"

That was what I feared most at this point. "I'll deal with it."

"You'll get thrown out on your ear."

Why did people keep using that term on me?

One night, a week or so later, Danica and I ate dinner on the screened-in back porch of Aunt June's house. A portable heat lamp warmed the area, while the breeze kept the air fresh and crisp—perfect combination. A large moon rose over the horizon. It was wintry and romantic.

"Did you seriously cook this?" Danica took another heaping spoonful of the fried rice in her bowl.

"That depends." I took a bite of the orange chicken. The candle on the table between us guttered. "Is it good?"

"It's delicious." She scooped another bite into her mouth before she'd even finished the last one. "And the candle on the table is such a nice touch."

"Candles make everything more special," I said. "Has anyone ever told you you're a very satisfying person to cook for? Never mind. Don't answer that."

A grain of rice remained on her lower lip, and she smiled. "You're finally catching on." Her eyes crinkled at their sides. "I'm a clean slate."

The grain of rice distracted me, and I couldn't stop staring at it. Danica lifted her hand and let it hover near her chin. "What? Is something wrong?"

"You've got a bit of—"

I touched my lower lip on the left side, mirroring her right where the offending item sat.

"Is there?" She touched the left side of her mouth, missing the rice. "Oh, no." She colored enough that I could see her blush by candlelight.

"Let me." I reached forward and brushed her lower lip with my thumb, and then placed the bit of rice in my napkin. "There. It's fine."

With her fingertips, she grazed the area. "I'm so embarrassed."

She shouldn't be. It'd given me a chance to touch the full lower lip of that perfect, tiny mouth. My fingers curled.

"Ever since you came by my house that day and burned me a

cheese sandwich, I've been trying harder."

"Harder to what?"

"Cook."

But there was no food in her cupboards. "Did you shop for ingredients?"

"My mom brought them by, based on a shopping list I gave her. I told her I was going to learn to cook." Danica set down her spoon. "Would you believe she gut-laughed?"

Yes. "That's not very nice."

"No, but it taught me something about my former self, and guess what? I don't want to be that person anymore."

My eyes flew open. "Yeah?" I maintained a casual tone, but my insides buzzed with swarms of a thousand bees of excitement. She wanted to leave some of her old ways behind. That meant everything to me. "Have you tried cooking anything yet?"

A little pout formed on that perfect mouth. "I'm going to need a coach."

I was so available for that. "Who have you got in mind? Is there a local cooking school in Wilder River I'm not aware of?"

A soft guffaw. "This is Wilder River." As in, *small towns have nothing exciting such as cooking schools.* "I was kind of hoping …" She lifted her large blue eyes to meet mine.

"Me?" I shook my head, even though my insides were singing triumphant superhero movie theme songs. "I'm much more of a businessman than a cook."

"You made this." To prove her point, she took a big bite of the orange chicken and spoke through it as she chewed. "It's incredible. Better than any restaurant. If I could remember restaurant food. Anyway, I know it tastes great. One dish? A signature dish, could you teach me?"

I sat back, as if contemplating, as if I needed an inducement. "I don't know."

"Please, Jeremy?" She batted her lashes and placed her hands flat beneath her chin. It was darling. "Maybe just a few fundamentals, then? I'd give you something in return."

"Something like what? I have almost everything I need." *Except Danica.*

"Name your price."

A kiss. Fifty kisses. A lifetime of a loving marriage. "Wash my truck?"

Her chin dropped. "You're kidding. I'm barely five feet tall. That thing might as well be a skyscraper."

"If you don't really want to learn to cook, then ..."

"No," she jumped to say. "I'll do it. Can it be at a carwash, driving through?" Her head wagged. "I guess not. It's a nice truck. It needs personal care."

Now, to be sure, I'd never hand-washed my own truck. The drive-through carwash was more than fine for that thing. But did I regret the image of Danica in car-washing clothes holding a hose and using a big carwash sponge?

No. I did not. "It's a deal." I held out my hand to shake on the terms.

She took it, but this time, she was the one to hold on a little longer. Our hands remained suspended over the table until the flame of the candle grew too hot on our wrists.

"Thanks, Jeremy." As if she were the one benefiting from the bargain. "You're really something special. I don't know how I'd manage this weird period of my life without you."

What about the rest of your life? Consider managing the rest of it with me, eh? "What ingredients did you have your mom purchase?"

We talked cooking, recipes, methods, and skills for a while.

"Seriously? I never knew there was a *no metal spoons in the Teflon pan* rule. Or such a thing as a silicone muffin pan. So that's how people get them out of the pans intact." She shook her head. "What *is* this dark magic?"

We finished dinner, and she loaded Aunt June's dishwasher while I scooped ice cream into cones.

"Let's go for a walk." She pulled my cone-free hand toward the front door.

A walk sounded fine to me, considering Aunt June had the TV volume set to *deafening*, and the night was cold but not prohibitively so.

Our steps crunched along the gravel drive, but we soon came to the well-worn sidewalk. The tree-lined street featured a few older houses and some large, empty lots begging to have houses built in them. Wilder River hadn't been overbuilt, despite the fact it was a resort town with all the attractions. The moon gave us most of our light, but we passed beneath streetlights now and then.

As we walked, Danica told me about the welcome back party at the gym, how weird she felt there not recognizing any of the kids. She also made the occasional comment about the town. "It's strange to walk down this street, and to know that somewhere in my brain is locked the history of the people who live here or there, and yet be unable to access it from the recesses of my mind. Instead, I'm stuck inventing histories for everyone."

"Such as?" I pointed to a two-story pink home with Victorian accents like a tower and a wraparound porch. "What about this house? Who lives here?"

"It has a sign on it—Peppermint Drop Inn. It's not fair if it's already named."

"Okay," I conceded. "What about that one?" I pointed next door, to a house without a placard naming it, and we walked toward it, basking in the lamplight.

After a thoughtful moment, she said, "That used to have a large family in it, but a cranky old man with too many cats bought it a few years ago. He tells the trick-or-treaters to stay off his lawn."

She pivoted and pointed next to a ranch-style house with dusty blue siding. "And that's where the school librarian lives. She has a puppy for whom she calls a sitter anytime she has to be in school. Her dream is to buy an RV and drive up the coastal highway next summer."

We resumed our walk.

"That's a good dream." My upper arm tingled as her shoulder bumped against mine. Then, she was leaning on me, and then, she'd slipped her arm through my elbow, linking us together. Maybe it was merely for steadiness on the uneven concrete of the aging sidewalk. I wasn't complaining. "What other histories have you invented? Anything about people in your life?"

"Just about you."

I caught myself from gasping. "Is that so?" I managed to say with a careless air. "Lay it on me."

"Oh, I don't think I should."

Neither did I, but suddenly, I was half feline—ready to be killed by my curiosity. "Fine. If you're too shy about it."

She gripped my arm tighter. "It's not that. It's …"

"No, it's fine." I waved it away, despite dying inside to know. "But if it would make you feel better, you can tell me a tiny aspect of it."

Danica kept walking, and she didn't say anything until we'd passed three well-lit houses. Then, she said softly, "You and I dated. In high school. We were each other's ideal match, but one of us got scared. Or there was a misunderstanding. We broke up, and you left Wilder River. I've never gotten over you, and that's why I never found anyone to marry. Your heart never let me go, and that's why you're here now."

Lava surged through my veins. My heart thundered like the bass drum in a Fourth of July marching band. "That's what you think?"

"No. It's what I invented. One of the scenarios."

"There are other scenarios?"

"Yeah, but they involve covert ops, submarines, alien life forms, or way too much bubblegum."

"I can see why you'd land on that first one to share with me."

"How close am I?" She stopped walking and turned to face me.

We stood beneath a streetlight, with the night insects swirling above us and a nighthawk swooping to get its evening feast.

"Some things aren't too far off." Like the part where she'd never left my heart. "Others, not even close."

Danica let out a heavy sigh. "I do appreciate the way you're not trying to force-feed me my past life."

"Is someone doing that?"

"Just my mom. I've been her family photo album hostage all week, with questions like *Don't you remember Uncle Jim? He was your favorite uncle. And here's your second cousin Veronica. You two used to go fishing all summer. You love fishing. Remember fishing?* It's sweet of her. I know she's really trying."

That sounded like torture. "Do you still *blank* fishing?"

"I don't know." She watched the nighthawk's soaring hunt for a bit. "Probably love? It sounds peaceful."

I turned us around to head back toward Aunt June's. We'd gone about a mile in our wanderings, and we'd almost come to the edge of this street's extent. "There's something I've been wanting to say to you." I needed to tell her the truth.

"Oh." She seemed so peaceful, too happy for what I'd originally planned to say. "What's that?"

I took her hand, and I laced my fingers through hers. "Your hand is small. Petite. Delicate. But it's also strong enough to do physical feats like gymnastics."

"That's what you wanted to tell me? Something about my hand?"

No. But it's what I'd said. I pressed my palm flat against hers, and we walked on. "You can look beyond the surface appearance of things and find the true strength."

"You're being a sphinx."

Actually, I was being a coward. What I wanted to say was that I was falling in love with her. With the Current Version of Danica, and that I suspected she was falling for me, too. "Answer my riddle, then, O traveler."

Danica gave a little laugh. "Pose thy riddle, O sphinx."

"What wilt thou cook first when I give thee thy lesson in thy

51

kitchen tomorrow at lunchtime?"

"I'll text you after I look through my recipe books."

Perfect. Ideal. "O be wise, what can I say more? Yes, I know what I can say more: nothing with truffle oil."

"Agreed."

"I'll try to clear my calendar." It was clear, or I'd clear it—other than my Army Reserve weekends. I couldn't wait.

Chapter 9

"I can't believe I made this soup!" Danica took another spoonful and then leaned her head back and sighed. "It's beyond delicious. Can we take a bowl to my mom? She'll flip out."

Her mom?

No.

Not a chance.

But it hit me that there was an important detail I didn't know yet. "Have you told her you're hanging out with me?"

"Sure. Of course."

My spine stiffened, but I relaxed it as quickly as possible. "How did she react to that?"

"What's the matter? Does my mom dislike you for some reason? Oh, no. Jeremy, did you dump me in the past and break my heart, and now my whole family despises you? Or, did I dump you and you refused to give up, and my family thinks you're a pathetic loser? Or—"

"I think that's enough scenarios." I handed her a napkin. "Chin."

She used the corner to remove the broth drip. "Thanks." She patted it a few more times and then gave me a snarky smile. "You didn't like my scenarios."

"I do like your soup." I took a bite. "And congratulations on making it all on your own." I'd stayed on the other side of the kitchen island, coaching from a distance. "You're quick to learn."

"I wish I could remember more people in my life. I feel like if I did, I'd take plastic containers of this soup to widows and shut-ins. I'd be going door-to-door checking on people, making sure they had what they need." A frown marred her visage. "But I can't remember anyone or anything they might need." Emotion crept into her tone. "Honestly, that feels like the biggest loss in all of this. That there are people I *know* need me, and I've left them hanging."

I set down my spoon and walked around to the chef's side of the island. I didn't gather her in my arms, though my every muscle ached to do so. "You've got the best heart, Danica."

"Is that why you're here? Because like attracts like?"

Was she saying I had a good heart? "And don't you forget it." I placed the flat of my hand gingerly at her hairline, and I lightly stroked her forehead with my thumb. "It's going to be all right, you know. Either you'll remember everything, or else you'll simply begin now to get to know everyone all over again, and you'll be able to love and serve them like you did before."

"Not exactly like I did before. Since I won't know all their history like I used to."

"In a way, can you see that as being a good thing?"

"Absolutely not." She straightened up and pulled my hand down. "The more you know a person, the better you can love them. If I know someone's hurts, I can begin to love them in spite of the negative behaviors that arise from the hurts. If I don't know the pain, and all I see is the jerky stuff people do, it's much harder to love. To know you is to love you, that's a song lyric, I think, and it's true. They're functionally equal."

I wanted to argue. But she was right that to know Danica was to love her. I loved her heart. The longer I spent with her, in close contact—and not just admiring her from afar as I'd done ever since I'd first offended her so egregiously that she'd cast me out—the more I grew to know her desires. Those hadn't changed, despite her forgetting everything else. She still desired to love and serve and protect her neighbors and her family members and the children she taught.

Everyone.

She was an angel.

"You said your sister is coming to town."

"It got postponed. She apparently had a surgery planned, and the date was moved up. I felt stupid for not knowing, so I didn't want to ask what kind of surgery, since everyone else on the video chat seemed to think I'd understand."

"Your sister was born with a bum leg."

Danica ran her palm down the side of her face, pulling at the skin. "No wonder!" She let out a *whoosh* of discovery. "That makes sense now. Thanks for telling me." She threw her arms around my waist. "Honestly, I should have you show up to everything with my family and whisper in my ear the background stories of things I'm missing. I seriously need a Sherpa to guide me through it."

I hardly heard the Sherpa part of her request, as all my neurons were standing at attention over the fact that Danica Denton had thrown her arms around me. Carefully, I placed my hands on her lower back, feeling the warmth of her body beneath my palms, and luxuriating in the pressure of her torso against mine. She rested the side of her head against my chest. "You're saying they don't get that you're suffering from amnesia?"

"I mean, they are aware, but they're not, at the same time. You know?" She released me, and I exhaled, but I also ached to reclaim her, to pull her into another embrace. "They can't quite comprehend it, I guess. There's so much assumption. And I'm left in the dark. It's tiring to keep having to ask, and I can tell it wears on them, too."

"So you've kind of quit asking, I take it."

She took a final mouthful of her soup and set the dish in the sink. "Would you? Come with me and translate all the stuff they're saying?"

Uh, not a great idea. "I wish I could." Truly. I wished that if I were to do so, they wouldn't cause a scene worthy of a Broadway musical.

About war. "They'll realize eventually what they're doing. It takes time."

"It didn't take you long." She reached across the island and caught the lip of my bowl to pull it toward her. She rinsed it and said, "You're different from everyone else, Jeremy. You're letting me take this at my own pace. I can't begin to tell you how much I appreciate it. How much I appreciate you." Her chin tilted upward, her eyes trained on mine, and she shut off the water and slipped her hands around my waist again. "I'm even excited to wash your truck."

She was as much as inviting me to kiss her. All of me wanted to. Every single cell, every atom in every cell. She nestled closer and rose up on tiptoe. Her hands pressed against the muscles of my back, pulling me closer, drawing me inexorably toward the target of her upturned mouth.

I want to. I can't. It's what I've dreamed of for ages. I can't. I can't. I can't.

"Would you go on a date with me, Danica? Dinner on Tuesday night?"

Chapter 10

Outside Wilder River by about three miles, the river bends so sharply and frequently that it reverses direction several times. There, the water slows to a near halt. Beside one bend, a stand of trees shades the edges, and there lies the best fishing in the county. Maybe in the state.

It was there I chose to take Danica on our first official date. Yes, we'd spent practically every day together since I came to town, other than my Reserve weekend, and we'd eaten dinner together every night for the past week as she expanded her cooking skills with varying levels of success. We were, for all intents and purposes, dating.

But I couldn't let it be misconstrued at any point. I couldn't let her old *you're such a good friend* phrase come back to bite me. I wanted to be clear. Crystal clear. I was dating Danica—because she wanted me to.

That afternoon, her text came. *Are you sure we can't get together before eight?*

She wanted to see me. My systems revved. *Why?*

If not, I have to put in an appearance on the family video chat, and you know how dreary those are for me. Please?

Begging. For my company. What other strange events would occur in life? Well, one I hoped for, absolutely—the kiss that I'd been saving for her all this time.

I took a swig of my Pepsi and formulated my response. *I'll try to come earlier, if I can. Wear a jacket and bring a coat. It's going to cool off tonight.*

The afternoon dragged on. It was all I could do not to tear out of Aunt June's driveway and speed to Danica's house and promise to whisk her away from all her troubles and cares, like she seemed to want me to do, and like I was more than capable of doing. Meanwhile, I raked up acorns and pecans on Aunt June's yard in advance of tonight's snow, raked some flowerbeds and covered them with corn stalks, moved stuff around in her garage, and repaired a couple of shingles on her shed.

Those tasks did not accelerate the clock.

"Hey, cousin." Garrett appeared. "You have plans for tonight? Some of us are getting together for a tailgate party before the last high school football game. I thought you'd like to paint yourself blue and reenact your finest hour."

Nice. "I'm figuring out better ways to impress girls."

"Like showing them the balance in your bank account instead, for instance?" Garrett snorfled. "Someone down at the plant told me about your latest major commercial property acquisition. Georgetown and Prince, wow. Two hundred units in the high rise? Impressive. They mentioned nine digits were involved. It's probably crass to ask, but was that *profit* to Houston?"

"Before taxes." I took off my work gloves and whacked him with them. "And you're correct. Anything that reminds me how much of life is eaten up by taxes is totally crass."

"You know me. Always saying the wrong thing."

"Ha." I rolled my eyes. "Ha, ha." If Garrett ever said the wrong thing in his life, no one had ever been around to hear it—as a twist on the *tree falls in the forest* postulate. "Have a good time tonight. Maybe you should paint yourself blue."

"I don't have the ripped body of a seventeen-year-old. It wouldn't be received with as much glee by the female population as when you did it."

"They were all covering their eyes."

"But peeking through their fingers. Man, of all the times I was jealous of you, that was the pinnacle."

Uh, no. "Be serious. That was the night of your biggest touchdown. Historic stuff."

Garrett just shrugged. "But who was everyone talking about the next day at school? And for the next six months?"

"The loser who humiliated himself for a girl and *still* got rejected?"

"Yep." The side of Garrett's face wrinkled. "Keep on keeping on, pal. She'll fall for you one day. But do consider flashing her the bank balance. It works every time, I'm told."

Garrett went inside, taking from his car a few grocery bags for Aunt June. He was a great guy. He ran the plant, he took care of his mom. How come Garrett hadn't fallen victim to one of the myriad girls in Wilder River who were likely pining for him? Or at least their mothers were pining that their daughters would snag him, for sure. *Why hadn't Danica chased him?*

The thought soured my saliva. I went for a drive to shake it off, playing the radio loudly, running the playlist of Australian boy band songs. Did I sing along? No one needs to know that. After a bit, I felt grounded again, and I went back to Aunt June's and gathered up all the supplies for the night's activity: two fishing rods, bait, a fish knife, plastic bags for our catch, blankets, folding chairs, dinner packed in a huge basket, flashlights, a lantern, and my courage.

I took them all to the river bend and set them up.

That prep took until seven forty-five, thank goodness. I headed to her house.

She rushed out to meet me. "You're early! Thank you. It got me off the video call just when they were passing around conflicting memories of events and breaking into an argument about who threw all the toilet paper down the outhouse hole when we went camping in the national forest when we were kids, and I just couldn't take another second of it. Thank you, Jeremy. You saved me once again. Ohh, it's dark."

"The moon will rise in a while." I helped her into the car, and she squeezed my hand, guiding it to stretch the seatbelt over her.

She wants me to touch her. I obliged, but I kept my mask of nonchalance fixed firmly in place.

We drove toward the edge of town. "What are we doing tonight for our first official date?"

"How do you know it's our first date?"

"Well, I don't, actually." She turned down the radio. "Be honest. Is this our first date?"

"Since you can't remember, let's just say it is. Let's start everything fresh, okay?"

"You make it sound like something had gone stale in the past." She pushed my bicep, but then she left her hand resting on it. "Although I can't imagine how it could have been. Every day with you has been pretty darn good. Maybe it's better I can't remember. I like the way things are going."

I suppressed all the welling emotion that made me want to slam on the brakes and yank her across the seat into my lap and kiss her for all I was worth. "Me, too," I said casually. "It's been pretty fun."

Pretty fun! Understatement of my life! It had been a constant roller coaster ever since I'd come back, always on the exciting downward slope of the track, one long, whizzing thrill fluttering my stomach and floating me through days and nights of elation. Like jumping out of a plane and never having to pull the chute.

I maneuvered off the edge of the road. A few hundred yards across a meadow of dried wildflowers lay the river, banked by the trees, and with the lanterns already lit.

"The full moon was a few days ago, so it should rise in a couple of hours."

"Will we get to watch it?"

"If we stay that long."

"Let's." She hopped out of the truck and into my waiting arms.

"It's such a beautiful night." She put her hand in mine and let me guide her to the less bumpy parts of the meadow. "Definitely great first-date material. It's fun to make a new memory. At least this time, I won't forget it."

Was that true? If she got her memories back, would these remain? I hadn't considered an alternative where they wouldn't. Nah, not how that stuff worked, right?

We arrived at my setup.

"Jeremy! No wonder you couldn't get together until eight. You were working on this all day." She thrust her arms around me. "It's amazing. You thought of everything."

The fishing rods leaned against the two sturdy, top-of-the-line lawn chairs, waiting for later. The lanterns glowed in the dimming twilight. Our dinner plates were covered by dome nets. It looked staged by a professional—and it had been. I'd called someone in the city and asked for photos and advice, starting on Wednesday right after Danica had said yes to the date.

Danica hugged me hard, her gymnast's strength and sinews at work. I liked it. A lot. More of that, please. "These lanterns are so pretty. Romantic. And they'll help draw the fish, I think, too. Right? I get the sense I've done that before." She gasped. "Do you think I'm getting a memory back?"

"Maybe." I helped her sit down on the plush blanket. "Right now, I'm more focused on creating new memories than recovering old ones." I took the dome off her dinner plate and set it aside. "Asparagus, a pork chop, and pasta with red sauce okay for you?"

"And strawberries." She took a ripe one from a bowl in the center and bit into it. "Mm. I think these are my favorite. Even more than raspberries." She ate another—a mesmerizing activity. I picked up a third berry and offered it to her.

Instead of taking it from me, she leaned over and ate it from my fingers.

Inside, I died on her altar again.

"Mmm," she moaned.

Uh-huh. Exactly.

My appetite for food fled. All I hungered for was Danica. "Should we fish a little first?"

I covered the food again. Then, we readied our poles and took the chairs down to the riverbank. There, we baited the hooks and both of us dropped lines in the water. The current gently tugged my line. We sat quietly, like good fishermen, and let the bait sink and the bobbers float. I caught a trout, and she caught two, probably the last of the season before the winter froze the river. It was great to see her excitement as she reeled in her catch. She even cleaned her own fish. Awesome. We stuffed the fishes into my tackle basket, wrapping them in plastic.

The fish must have moved on, though, because there were no bites for a while. Danica sat beside me on my upstream side. Her chair was on uneven ground, though, and when she leaned forward, it toppled, landing hard against my side.

"Oh! Jeremy!"

Instead of pushing her backward, I pulled her toward me, tugging her across the arm rest and into my lap. "You need a safer place to be."

She nestled against me, leaning her back against my chest. "You're a hundred percent accurate. In every sense."

"And do you think of me as that safe place, Danica?" I whispered into her ear that was so near to me.

"Yes and no."

"Explain?"

"I'm utterly comfortable around you. I feel totally safe with you emotionally. Like I can be every bit myself, whatever that means, and you're not judging me or asking me to be what I used to be or what I ought to be. You take me where I am. It's the safest thing I can imagine."

"But?"

"But physically? I'm in mortal danger." Then, in a move that can only be described as acrobatic, Danica wrested around, hooking her legs beneath mine, while twisting her upper torso toward me and wrapping me in a strong embrace. "Danger of something like this."

Danica Denton offered her full, perfect, pouting, delicious mouth to me. With the slightest pressure, she brushed those lips against mine, igniting every millimeter of contact. My skin flamed to life, doused in the lighter fluid of a lifetime of wanting this, of wanting *her*. Of wanting Danica to want me.

With deft skill, she coaxed my mouth into a full kiss, and then delved deeper, an exploratory operation, and soon, I was putting up no fight against her insistence. In fact, I took over as lead of the mission, and in no time, we were diving into uncharted territory. And it had come with a few weeks still to go before Christmas, in fact.

Early Merry Christmas to me—it was all my holiday wishes come true at once.

Meanwhile, this was no simple physical exercise, though I was definitely getting an aerobic workout as the kiss progressed from seconds into minutes. No, this was a connection, a piecing together of lost parts of my soul that Danica had been hanging onto all this time and was now inserting to complete the full picture of who I was, and who I could be—with her.

I never thought it could be this good. I'd never imagined anything so passionate that could also be so emotional at the same time. Movies and books never portrayed anything this multifaceted. But as Danica's kisses trailed across me and her hands traced my musculature, there was nothing one-dimensional about the experience. It was spherical, and expanding.

And I was getting close to falling onto one knee right here and proposing—before anything could ever go wrong.

"I'm falling for you, Jeremy."

Yeah? Well, I fell for you the minute you defended me when I first moved to Wilder River. You told all the kids to back off and quit bullying the new kid for being weird and hyper. You spotted a fresh, untended can of Pepsi and snatched it. You thrust the can into my hands. "Drink this. It'll calm you down. I know." And it did. And I was yours from that moment on.

However, instead of that tumult of admissions, all I said was, "It's getting pretty real over here, too." I pushed her hair back off her face and kissed her neck until she made a sound that let me know we'd moved into actually dangerous territory.

"We should finish our dinner. We missed the moonrise, but in a half hour, the Perseids will be visible."

"The meteor shower?" Danica's breath came quickly. "Is it that late? Time flies." She gave me one more luxurious kiss. "If you want to go on another official date soon, I'm free tomorrow night as well."

I'd make time.

Chapter 11

"We didn't catch many fish last night." Danica unloaded her tennis racquet from behind the seat of my truck. "But I like what we caught instead." The tone of her voice hinted at our kissing session.

She'd found a pair of racquets in her hall closet at home and had asked to try them out and see whether she was actually a tennis player. Muscle memory would tell her. I was game for that. And for Danica in a tennis skirt.

We crossed the snowy parking lot, headed for the town rec center's indoor court, and she skipped beside me as I walked. A town like Wilder River needed as many indoor recreational opportunities as possible, with winter dominating the year.

Danica grabbed my hand and swung it, and then she jumped onto the bench seat just inside the court. Standing on it, she gave me a good, solid kiss. "It's driving me crazy not to be cleared to return to work yet. What were you doing all morning that you couldn't come rescue me from my boredom?"

"You were bored?"

"Dreadfully." She talked about going to the gym and staring at the kids' faces to try to remember their names—with no luck.

"You needed more *Jane Eyre*."

"I needed more Jeremy Houston." She wrapped her legs around

my waist, and before I knew it, I was spinning her around. She whipped out her phone and took a selfie of us in that ridiculous but mind-blowingly good embrace. Then she sent it to me. "So you can remember this moment. The first time we kissed in a tennis court."

We played a couple of sets. She was a lot better at it than I was, and eventually she took pity on me. "If you don't play tennis, what do you do?"

"In my profession, golf is more the standard."

"Oh, I think … I think I still *love* golf. Can we try it?"

The next afternoon, the sun had come out and melted most of the first snowfall, so we golfed. The full front nine, she beat me. Sorely. "Are you okay with that?"

"I love a challenge."

She sidled up to me on the golf cart, her leg pressing against mine and her arm around my waist. "And am I a challenge?"

Gracious, she had no idea. "If I say you are, will you extrapolate *if A then B, if B then A?*"

"I might." She proceeded to challenge me at golf on the back nine. And by flirting with me outrageously. By saying whoever scored lower on the hole got to choose the length of that hole's kiss in the golf cart.

Our golf cart saw more kissing action than it had probably seen in years. If ever. Danica set the kiss timer longer each time she won. And that was every time.

Not that I was losing anything here. Believe me. Nobody won more by losing at golf that day than I did, even someone who'd been bribed to throw the Master's Tournament. It was becoming clearer to me minute by minute that I was going to have to either propose to this woman and make her mine forever or—

Or tell her the truth about our past and watch her stomp out of my life. Again.

I opted for a step toward the former.

The sun sank toward the horizon. "It's probably time to return the golf cart," I said between rounds of kissing her behind the clubhouse, in the shade of the evergreens. "Unless you want me to just buy it."

"Yes." She went back to kissing me. "I'll want one for each day of the week."

I succumbed to this faulty reasoning.

A few passion-filled minutes later, I rallied my willpower again. "If we go now, I can make you dinner."

"I don't need food. I don't need air." She kissed me again, and then she started to crawl onto my lap. Like, as if this was going somewhere else.

Much as it felt like the right plan, I knew it wasn't. Not yet. I twisted to block her move, but I met her gaze and said soberly, "Danica. I've been crazy about you for as long as I can remember." The admission felt like all the water of Niagara Falls flowing off me in one giant splash. "You're all I've thought of."

Her blue eyes filled up, glossy and yet happy. "As weak as this is going to sound, it's the same for me about you, Jeremy. For as long as I can remember, I've wanted you. The second you showed up in my hospital room, I thought I was the luckiest woman alive if a gorgeous man like you would appear with four bouquets for me, and then, when you read me my favorite book, I was a goner. Hook, line, and sinker. Or at least I thought that was as gone as I could be over you—then you kissed me. Speaking of hooks, lines, and sinkers."

She kissed me again, and I let all this information swirl through me. For once I didn't want to scale back my reaction to her, for once I wanted to break loose and tell her all I was feeling. But she interrupted my confession with another round of kisses, and then a soul-melting speech.

"Your kiss is my life's breath. I can't—I can't anything without it. Without you. I know this is gushing. I know it's over the top, but all these weeks I've been waiting for some declaration from you, and I guess my dam just broke. It's like I have to tell you everything I'm feeling. How much I'm wanting you. Wanting us. Wanting this. Whatever happened before, I'm just—let's forget it. I know I already have. Over and over, you've argued for the merits of fresh starts. Well, I'm all for them. Not just because I have no choice in the matter. I'm in love with you, Jeremy. You make me feel like nothing else matters but you and me and the two of us and who we are and what we can build together in this life." And this time, she did crawl into my lap, and I let her nestle there, with my arms around her, secure and safe, and almost permanent.

The sun had set, and the last employee came around the back of the clubhouse. His name tag read *Rufus*.

"There you are." Rufus gave us a scolding look. "You were supposed to return that cart by four. The next group who'd reserved it had to walk." He muttered something that sounded like, *"Of course, they needed the exercise, if you ask me."* Then, he shooed us out of the cart and drove it back to the golf cart corral.

I waited for his return and shook his hand. "Sorry for the inconvenience. I'll call tomorrow and pay for the extra time."

"Your credit card has already been charged, Mr. Houston." So Rufus knew me. Or at least he'd seen my name on the roster of cart rentals. "Don't worry, we didn't overcharge you just because of the Georgetown and Prince acquisition. Though don't think we didn't consider it. You can afford to buy your own golf cart, man. A whole fleet of them."

Good point.

In the truck on the drive back to Danica's place, she asked, "What was Rufus saying about golf carts and Georgetown?"

"Georgetown is a neighborhood in Washington, D.C." I sounded so stupid right now. "I'm guessing they have a nice golf course or two there, to keep the politicians happy."

"Jeremy." Danica was having none of my obfuscation. "Fine. I'll look it up online. I'll look *you* up online." She whipped out her phone.

"You mean you haven't done that already?"

"I was allowing you the courtesy of revealing yourself through what you wanted to share with me."

That was noble. Something few people in this world would do these days. "I appreciate it."

She put her phone away and turned to look at me pointedly. I rolled us up to a drive-through burger place. "Do you want cheese on your burger?"

I ordered through the intercom for us both, and then, when we had our paper sack of dinner, I pulled over at the town park. From here, the whole ski resort was visible, and at the top of the hills, the recent snow reflected in the starlight.

We found a picnic table, and I handed her a cheeseburger. "I have a company in the city. It's been really successful, especially lately. A deal we did last month got a lot of publicity in commercial real estate sales circles, and a little beyond them."

"Oh? Go on." She took a big bite of the burger and chewed, allowing me time to gather more thoughts.

"And I will probably need to wind up my time here in Wilder River pretty soon and get back to my responsibilities there." At least by the end of November. There were contracts to sign in person.

"You're leaving?"

"I mean, eventually, yeah."

"By eventually, do you mean before the end of the year? Before the end of the week?"

I laughed and placed my index finger on her nose. "Eventually is eventually. We'll go skiing or snowmobiling first, though. For sure."

"Jeremy." Her brows pushed together, and she rewrapped her burger, as though it no longer appealed. "I guess I thought ..."

She'd assumed I was staying in Wilder River, clearly.

If only I could.

Chapter 12

"Jeremy. You missed another great tailgate party." Garrett tossed me a cold can of Pepsi from Aunt June's fridge.

"I thought football was done. And it snowed a foot yesterday afternoon. "

"It is done, but basketball started." He took a can of something else. "We winter climate people. We can party outdoors in the worst temperatures. Build us a bonfire, and we're good to negative ten."

"Loony toons, that's what you all are."

"I heard from Rufus you were busy stealing golf carts from the clubhouse instead of enjoying franks on the barbecue with us. Always in trouble. Always. Even when you can afford to buy your own golf cart. It's ridiculous, don't you think? The trouble that girl gets you into?"

"Danica is so much trouble." I popped the top of the can, and the hiss of carbonation escaped. Tiny bubbles pinged against my lip as I sipped the cola-flavored nectar. "More like Danica is *in* so much trouble."

"Did she get arrested for stealing the cart? Or—wait. You're saying she's into you? No. Dude! Really?" He pounded my back hard enough that a slosh of Pepsi splashed onto my hand. "All this time, and you're finally going for it. I bet her family isn't too happy about it. What do her parents say, or are they keeping out of it because Danica's been injured?"

What Garrett said was a possibility. They might be giving Danica a wide berth since she'd been hurt.

"She mentioned me, but when they reacted, I think she stopped talking about us to them. If she does tell them everything, though, do you think they could chalk it up to her memory loss and be happy for us?" My voice grew thin at the end of the question.

"Jeremy, do you *remember* her sister's wedding?"

I bit my lips together and closed my eyes.

"I see you haven't forgotten. The swan sculpture, the swimming pool covered with floating candles in Christmas wreaths, you on the motorcycle in the black leather jacket with Danica's name embroidered on it."

"I admit, I was going through a phase. But to be fair, Penelope is the one who told me that women crave a grand gesture to prove their love. She was studying romance novels back in her days of wanting to be an author. Thank goodness that ended." Now, Penelope was a full-time mom and a part-time perfumer, with her own signature scent she sold online. Quite successfully, too. Her kids got the bulk of her attention, though. "Look, I am going to choose to believe that those good people in the Denton family are capable of overlooking adolescent follies and of trusting their adult daughter's decisions about whom she chooses to love."

"Whom." Garrett guffawed. "All the grammar has been unleashed." He shook his head. "Are you sure she's into you?"

"Finally, Garrett. After all this time, she is giving me a chance. She really, honestly likes me." I almost said *loves*. "It's the best thing that's ever happened to me."

"She likes you, but does she *know* you?"

"I think so."

"Have you thought this through? What if she *does* love you? What will her family do?"

"They'll take it in stride," I said, though I hadn't actually thought

71

through the possibility of her loving me and all the implications. The reminder of her family's disgust for me was a kick in the gut.

"If you ask me, you're playing with fire."

I was. He had no idea how fiery things got between Danica and me on a regular basis.

"And with a girl's feelings. A good girl. A girl who is at a major disadvantage unless you enlighten her."

When he put it that way, I did feel like a heel. "I'll tell her. In my own way."

"Better not delay. If things are moving as fast as Rufus hinted, you're either soon to be married by choice or by the tip of her dad's shotgun."

"It's not *that* much fire." But it was close. Garrett was right.

Then, he sobered. "Honestly, Jeremy. She's a very nice girl. She deserves someone who tells her the whole truth. Don't play her."

He stalked away.

I set down my Pepsi, the taste of it suddenly tasting metallic against my tongue.

***

"I love it when you make me dinner." Danica wrapped her arms around my waist as I stood at the stove in her kitchen. She rested her head against my back, and her heartbeat pulsed through to my spine. It felt so right, the way we fit together every way we'd touched. "I still owe you that truck-washing for teaching me to make orange chicken and all those other things. Though it's getting pretty cold for that now. Can I give you a raincheck for after the spring thaw?"

She pictured us together in the spring? "I guess so."

She giggled. "Tonight I have a surprise, though."

"Yeah?" I salted the chicken and added a little more butter beneath where the meat met the pan. "What's that?"

"I made dessert." She let go of me and bounced toward the fridge, where she opened the freezer and took out a cake, layered with ice cream. "It's nowhere near as amazing as the thing you brought the other

72

day with the strawberries and the pretzels, but I had to start somewhere, right? See? I followed all the directions in the cookbook. I even sifted the flour and the other dry ingredients together. I made a cupcake with some excess batter, and when I tasted it, it worked! You were so right! Anyone can cook, even me." She put it back in the freezer. "I will admit that I bought the ice cream, though, for the layers. Is that cheating?"

"Ice cream was an ingredient in the recipe, right? So it's fine. You simply added the ingredient."

Her eyes softened, as if I was a guru and had just given her a key to happiness. "You're so right. You're always so right. So right for me." She wedged herself between me and the stove for a minute.

We ate dinner, played a round of backgammon, which I won, for once, and then I read her another chapter in *Jane Eyre*. She could read herself by now, obviously, but she asked if I would read to her anyway.

I obliged.

"There's someone in the attic?" Danica gasped when I read that reference. "Oh, my gosh! Who is it? It's not a ghost, is it? Is someone alive?" She was on the edge of the couch, leaning toward me.

I set my phone with the book's text face down on the coffee table, which was an arm's length away. "We'll read more about it after we've had dessert."

She clearly knew I wasn't referring to the cake she'd made, because she leaped forward and landed on top of me, giving me the beginnings of a passionate kiss—in a not-so-safe position.

I scooted to the side a little, to give her more room, and to extract myself from more danger than I was ready to endure, and beneath me, the sofa cushion shifted. We were falling.

The inexorable power of gravity took control of both of us. I clutched Danica, but at the same time, she rolled—toward the edge of the couch, and soon—*whump!*

We were on the slats of the hardwood floor. Me, on top of her. Danica facing up, her eyes squeezed shut, as if in atrocious pain.

"What made that awful sound?" In a flash, I was off her, standing to help her to her feet. "Danica? Are you okay? Did I hurt you?"

Slowly, her eyes cracked open. Discernment filled them, and she stared up at me. "Did you hurt me? Jeremy?"

"Come on. Let me help you up." I extended my hand, and I bent to lift her.

Danica just looked at my hand like it was a piece of rotting fish. "Jeremy Houston, what in the world are you doing in my house? And on top of me?" She rubbed the back of her head.

"Danica?" I asked, my voice smaller than it had been in years. "Danica."

"You'd better get yourself out of here before I call the police. I'm pretty sure there was no expiration date on that restraining order I requested against you at Angelica's wedding. Get out. Get. Out." Her voice was low, menacing, and serious as death.

"Good-bye." I dusted myself off, picked up my keys and jacket, and closed her door softly behind me as I left.

The jig was up.

Part II: Chapter 1

Danica

I sat in abject horror on my floor for the longest time, just processing.

Had I been drugged and taken hostage in my own home by my most hated enemy as revenge for ... something I'd done in the past?

Had I been in one of those dissociative fugues from psychological thriller novels where I did a whole bunch of irrational and unthinkable things against my moral code while I was awake and then forgot about them?

Nothing made sense. Jeremy Houston had been in my house, looking at me like *that*. Like I'd mortally wounded him.

And like *that*. Like handsome. *Why was my body chemistry reacting to his physicality that way?*

I lifted the front of my sweater to my nose and sniffed. A man's cologne lingered there.

Something terrible had obviously happened.

And I needed three extra-strength Tylenol tablets, pronto.

"Mom?" I dialed her number while I filled my water glass. The kitchen was a holy terror of a mess. Dishes everywhere, cooking spatters on the stovetop, a small splash of olive oil at the base of the oil vessel.

Since when did my kitchen have all these pots and pans and ingredients?

"Sweetheart, you missed our family video chat. We were talking about Angelica's surgery."

Angelica! Her hip surgery to lengthen some tendons and shorten others. In the planning works for months and months, it was supposed to help her walk better. "How is she doing? Is she healing up?"

"Honey, the operation was postponed until tomorrow. You know that. Are you still planning to come to Reedsville and see her in the hospital? You can't drive yet, and you said someone was bringing you. Someone you wanted us to meet."

My mind spun, and I tilted my head sideways to see whether the world had rolled over on its axis.

"Danica? Sweetie? Are you all right? You're being very quiet."

"This is going to come out of nowhere, Mom, but do you remember Jeremy Houston?"

"Who could forget that lunkhead?" Some muttering ensued. "No matter why you've been bringing him up again lately, I swear, if I ever run into him in a dark alley, his minutes are numbered. Do you *recall* how he destroyed your sister's wedding—and our newly laid turf in the back yard—with his motorcycle? Which he obviously had no idea how to ride. Even his sister screamed in his face for that."

Yeah, Penelope had been particularly shrill with him. It'd made all the rest of us in the wedding party step back and let her handle him. She'd escorted him off the property, in lieu of my dad calling the police.

"I'll never forget how that carved ice swan looked, floating upside down in the swimming pool." I shook my head. Jeremy Houston was a total buffoon.

My home had a strict *no buffoons allowed* policy. So what had he been doing there?

"Why do you ask about Jeremy? Please tell me he's not been on television as one of America's Most Wanted. I always knew he'd come to a bad end. No impulse control, that one."

"I think he just had ADHD, Mom." Now, there I went, defending him. Again. Like I'd done for him to my family so many times in the past—at least until that final prank. The one that made him dead to me. "I saw him today, that's all. It'd been a long time. And no, he wasn't wearing an orange jumpsuit or anything." But he would be if he tried to set foot in my house uninvited again. That lunkhead! Mom's term was so apropos.

"Well, don't let his negativity distract you from your good news. You're not going to give me even the tiniest hint of who you were bringing to meet us? Pretty please?"

"Mom, you know I love giving a good surprise." I gracefully exited the conversation, tamping down my concern. What had Mom meant, I was bringing someone? As if. Unless it was more of her wishful thinking that I'd throw myself at Garrett Bolton.

Not happening. He was nice, a great guy, youngest ever foreman at the plant, but ...

Instead, I went into the kitchen to recover it from whatever hurricane had wreaked havoc.

First, I loaded the dishwasher with anything dishwasher-able. Then, I came to the pan on the stove. Curdled bits of browned meat lined the edges. I picked one free and tasted it. Mmm. That was *good.* I picked out a bit more. Then, looking around, I found a dinner plate with half a chicken breast remaining, golden brown and still juicy. Oh, wow. This was incredible. Probably the best thing that had ever happened in this kitchen.

In no time, it was gone, as were the greens beside it, so buttery and garlicky and good. What else was in this kitchen? I opened the fridge. Whoa. Who'd stocked this thing? Every food group was in there! I cracked open plastic storage containers of leftovers and sampled each of them. Oh, my lands. These were amazing. What the heck was going on here? In my dissociative fugue state, had I suddenly learned to cook?

I popped a piece of bread into the toaster and in the microwave reheated some kind of sauce from the fridge. When the toast popped up, it was burnt. Like, set off the fire alarm level. Yeah, that was more like my skill set. And then, a loud *pop!* sounded from the microwave. The lid had blown off the Tupperware and the sauce dripped from every surface inside the little oven.

Yeah, this was a *lot* more like my cooking skills.

Obviously, someone else had been inhabiting this house. I sounded like one of the three bears right now: who's been cooking in my kitchen?

No more attempts at snacking. I finished cleaning up the mess and then wiped down all the counters and the inside of the microwave oven. My head was hurting—a lot. I opened the freezer to find an ice pack for the back of my head, or a bag of frozen peas, or—

What was that? A cake? With ice cream as the center layer?

Joy. Joy. Joy!

In no time flat, I was devouring the piece of cake I'd cut for myself. Mmm. Creamy, chocolaty, sweet, bitter, delicious, amazing. Who had made this? The person was a baking genius.

Why do I feel like I made it?

Because of wishful thinking, obviously. No way on earth could I bake something. I should be prohibited from setting foot in kitchens other than to procure the odd glass of water or juice.

I took one more slice of the cake and put the rest back in the freezer. Genius to layer it with the ice cream. The Dairy Queen herself had been visiting, apparently. With a sigh, I wandered to the living room and put on some music and ate the cake slowly. Soon, my head stopped throbbing. Chocolate has healing properties, I swear.

I should call Angelica and wish her luck with her surgery. Unfortunately, I took a huge bite of cake as I dialed, and she answered before I could swallow.

"Danica?" Angelica said tentatively through the phone. "Are you doing all right? I've been so worried."

Finally, I muscled down the cake. "I'm the one who's worried about you," I sputtered. "Tell me all the details of your upcoming surgery. Is it really happening? Are you emotionally prepared? What can I do to help? I'll come down to Reedsville, stay at your house, be your live-in physical therapist, feed your dog. Anything you need."

"Danica!" she stage whispered. "You're back!" Squealing ensued, and a fair bit of threatening to call Mom with the news, and a whole bunch of other stuff I didn't really follow.

It must have something to do with my blank-out for the past couple of hours. Long enough to go shopping and fill my fridge, to hire someone to cook dinner, and to temporarily go insane enough to allow Jeremy Houston to set foot in my house. I'd put it at six hours.

"And so, I told Brady, my husband in case you forgot, that I was praying for you, and he said you'd come back to yourself any day now and not to worry too much because worrying was putting too much negativity into the stratosphere, and I said is that where negativity lives, or is it a different layer of the atmosphere, and he got all philosophical, and then he said it's fine if I pray harder, as long as I quit worrying all the time, and now, voilà! You're yourself again!"

"Yay," I said halfheartedly. What was that diatribe supposed to mean? How long had I *not* been myself? Hadn't it just been a matter of hours? I ripped my phone from my ear and moved to the home screen, which should display the date and time.

What? November? *Late* November? Almost Thanksgiving? My stomach clenched. I rested a hand on my abdomen, where the muscles felt weaker than usual. How was my strength elsewhere? I tested a few muscle groups. Definitely soft.

"Angelica?" My voice trembled. "I feel like something's off."

"It's not off. Not anymore. You're *back*. And as soon as my surgery is over, you and I are—I don't know—signing up for a sisters cruise. Brady won't mind. He's been really worried about you, just like the rest of us."

A chunk of time two calendar pages long was missing from my

life. *Now* was the time they should be worrying about me. My breath started to come in large gulps. "I have to call you back."

"Just whenever. Love you, sister." Angelica hung up, just in time for me to race to the back yard, where a bracing blast of fresh air entered my lungs. When had it turned cold? I'd missed most of fall. I love autumn. It was now full-on winter, if the scent of wood-smoke in the air was my guide.

In the distance, a skiff of snow decorated the top of the mountain with the ski resort already. This was *too* weird. Too terrible.

I needed help. But who could tell me what was going on? It was like I had amnesia or something.

The door bell rang. I went back in the house and answered the front door, bracing myself to see someone I didn't recognize, or another face from my distant past like Jeremy's. What person had I become in the past couple of months?

Instead, it was Tennille. "Danica." Tennille came bursting into the house, her arms full of black plastic bags. "You're not going to understand this, I'm sure, but no matter what's been going on, I feel like I at least have to okay the costumes for the holiday recital with you." She opened the top of one of the bags and dumped the contents onto my sofa. "Oh, I wish you could understand all this. I'm drowning in paperwork. The lawyer just keeps shoving it at me. He didn't"—she looked at the floor and then the ceiling—"mail you anything, did he?"

"Lawyer?" I rubbed the back of my head. Tennille's voice sounded like it was coming at me down a metal tube. "I haven't received anything from a lawyer."

She exhaled and looked around the room. "It's messy in here." Her gaze landed on the table. "What's that dinner plate? It looks like chicken. Did you cook? Girl, you're really changing."

"I—do you want to try it? It's pretty good." I brought the plate I'd missed while doing dishes to her and held up a forkful of the chicken. "If you like chicken."

I said this with a little smirk. Tennille loved chicken. It was her favorite food. She went to every chicken place when we traveled for gymnastics competitions with the older kids. We never went for seafood or beef or vegetarian. Always, always chicken.

"Mmm." Her eyes rolled back in her head as she chewed. "This is divine. Oh, my stars. The buttery goodness of it. What's your recipe? I *must* have it." She shifted into one of those acting voices for the last bit and rubbed her hands together. "Out with it."

I turned to the costumes. "Show me what you've got. Are these for the four- to six-year-olds?"

"Yep." Tennille stepped between me and the pile of fabric and sequins. "But stop the presses. You can't tell me this food is something you're keeping secret. Out with it. No takeout place in Wilder River makes anything this good. Did *you* cook it?"

That was just it. I had no idea. "I guess?"

"What do you mean, you guess? You're *Danica Denton*. Drive-through Danica, who eats take-out seven days a week. The woman who burns water."

"Right?" That was my puzzle as well. "This is going to sound utterly bizarre, but I can't remember if I cooked it."

"You mean your amnesia has yanked your short-term memory as well?"

"What's that supposed to mean?"

With a know-it-all demeanor, she perched on the arm of the couch and folded her arms over her chest. "Do you remember my coming to the door a few minutes ago?"

"What is this, Tennille? Of course I do. You're sitting right here."

"What were you doing right before that?"

"I was getting some fresh air in the back yard." Trying to stop my hyperventilation. "It's snowy at the top of Mount Wilder already. Did you notice?"

With squinty eyes she searched me. "And before that?"

"I talked on the phone with Angelica. And before that, with my mom. What, are you tracing my life backwards now?"

81

"Exactly. And what happened before you talked on the phone with your mom?"

Oh. That. That was the part that got fuzzy. "I—well, I kicked Jeremy Houston out of my house." I shoved the bottoms of my palms into my eyes and scrunched up my face. "What in the heck was Jeremy Houston doing here? That's insane, right?" I pulled down my hands and looked at Tennille to confirm the insanity. "That had to be an apparition. Jeremy couldn't have been here. I must have hit my head."

Indeed, the back of my head did hurt. I patted it gently, and there was a growing lump.

Tennille eyed me. Hard. "You … know me."

I rolled my eyes. "Look, I don't know what you're doing. But stop. I've got a blossoming headache and a mysterious chicken dinner and"—I yanked my sweater's neckline in front of my nose for a second—"Jeremy Houston's cologne on my shirt." I made a gagging sound. "I am in no mood for shenanigans from my business partner. My brain is playing enough of them on me as it is."

Instead of giving me more stinky looks, Tennille thrust her arms outward, lunged at me, and gathered me into a huge hug. "This is the best day ever!" She jumped up and down as she hugged me, jarring my brain inside my skull. "Oh, man. Can I tell you what a relief this is? I have been having the hardest time figuring out all the business decisions by myself. It's been crazy. If I ever start getting ungrateful, just stop me. You do so much for Candy Cane Cottage, and I honestly had no idea before, and"—she pulled back and looked at me at arms' length—"and I'm just so glad to see you again."

"Thanks." I pulled out of her grasp. "But could you dial down the rejoicing and tell me what's going on?"

"Sure, but I just registered what you said a minute ago. Jeremy Houston was here—and your sweater smells like him. Yikes, much?"

"*Much* yikes." I shuddered. That buffoon—and why did I smell like him? I hated so much that I had no idea.

"You called the cops, I hope."

"No, he made himself scarce the second I told him to get out. But the weird thing is, he looked just as much like a martyr today as when I banished him from Angelica's wedding."

"I guess some people never change. Poor sucker."

"What does that mean?"

"It means, what the heck is he doing in Wilder River, hanging around you when you obviously hate his guts? Man, I swear, I thought once he moved away and made a hundred million dollars, he'd emotionally move on from this place. I mean, I would."

Hundred million dollars. What? Not Jeremy Houston. That goof-off probably didn't have a hundred dollars, let alone a hundred million. "Nah, your heart is here forever." Not that I'd know about Jeremy's doings over the past decade. I ignored all gossip concerning him, and people had eventually stopped trying to force-feed it to me.

"Yeah, seems like Jeremy's was, too." Tennille smirked. Then, she launched into an explanation that was harder to hear than a first-year violin student's practice.

An explanation about me, an accident, the hospital, and a bad outcome that had lasted two months.

"You're joking." I coughed on my reaction. More like choked. "I didn't have amnesia. No way."

"Two months ago. It was awful, seeing you at the base of the uneven bars. I called the ambulance. You were out cold."

When she mentioned the uneven bars, the moment came crashing back on me. I recalled the falling sensation, but nothing after that. "Please say no students saw my lifeless body on the ground." We'd have to organize trauma counseling or something. Moms would be pulling their kids from the program en masse. "What happened afterward to everyone else?"

Tennille smiled. "That's just like you, Danica. Always worried about how other people are affected. You didn't even ask about your ambulance ride or the hospital stay or anything. Of course, that's probably stuff you remember."

Uh, no. "Believe it or not, I'm drawing a blank on everything from the moment of the accident until …"

"Until you woke up with Jeremy Houston's cologne wafting all around you? Friend, you had better *never* take up drinking. You're just the type who would run off to a Vegas wedding while drunk and wake up pregnant in a hotel room with who-knows-whose baby."

I recoiled. "No, I wouldn't. Even when incapacitated, I still have a moral compass."

Tennille placed her hands on her hips and raised an eyebrow of accusation. "Sweater evidence?"

Fine. "Well, that must have been a lapse. There had to be a good explanation. Did you see him with me during that time?"

"Just once."

What! "You … Why didn't you lead with that?" Geez, some friend. "You knew I was brainless, you saw me with Jeremy Houston and didn't—I don't know—step in and save me from his evil designs?"

"You were in a fragile state, okay?" Tennille looked at her nails. "And let's be real. He's a goofball, but not *dangerous*. Those are two different things altogether. Plus, when you were kicking him out, did you catch a glimpse of him? Hotter than asphalt on a summer day in Phoenix." She fanned herself.

"I didn't look." Oh, but I had. I'd looked—long enough to realize Jeremy Houston was one of the better-looking men I'd ever seen. And my body had reacted to his presence quite strongly. It was reacting now, too, as I recalled his face and form.

But that hurt look on his face put a halt to my rising tide of whatever that was for him. Whammo. Done.

"You didn't look. Ha," Tennille snickered. "From what I heard, you spent quite a bit of time with him. Someone saw you playing tennis together."

"Tennis!" I hadn't played tennis in ten years. I rushed to the front hall closet, expecting to have to dig my racquets out from behind the coats and the suitcase. "They're on the top of the snow boots," I said.

Tennille was at my shoulder. "And they're not dusty." I turned to her. "Anything else?"

"Golf."

Golf? "Do I golf now?" I took a golf class in college, thinking I'd be able to use those skills if I got my MBA, but I'd stopped with a bachelor's degree in business, because that had been when the opportunity came up to buy the building my third great-grandmother had owned. "I golfed with Jeremy Houston? Was anyone else there? Were we being coached by Tiger Woods?"

"Um, no. The only person doing the coaching was *you*. And according to Rufus Swalwell, you were coaching Jeremy on the finer points of a different kind of game while you were parked in a golf cart behind the clubhouse."

Stop. I shoved my hands over my ears, letting a tennis racquet clatter to the tile floor and another one land atop my bare foot. Ouch on all fronts. "This is just—no. Who am I? And what have I done with Danica Denton?" Much more than amnesia going on. "Was I *possessed* or something? Am I a changeling? Should we call a priest and have an exorcism done?"

My nose started running, and my eyes pricked. What had Jeremy Houston been doing back in Wilder River, anyway? If only I could squash him like a bug.

Tennille gave me a maternal hug. "You're going to be fine. You're yourself again." She patted my back.

That was the second time I'd heard that phrase tonight. It shouldn't feel this unsettling.

"Let's go look through the costumes. You can give me your approval, and then tomorrow, you can come into Candy Cane Cottage and help me pass them out to the kids. The holiday extravaganza is in three weeks, on Saturday afternoon."

Our winter showcase already! Well, I had better resume my life. She was right.

But what had I done to destroy my life in the meantime?

Chapter 2

At the end of the last practice right before Thanksgiving, all the kids and moms gathered around me. The air in Candy Cane Cottage was warm from the heater, and I'd found the gym's Christmas tree all dusty in the storage room, and I'd popped it up. Now it could feel holiday-ish in here—even though it did all year long, what with the candy cane stripes going on even in summer.

The kids each took a costume. I loved the smiles on their faces when they received their assigned colors. Some were red, others where white, and the last group were green. Christmas festive. The sequins were the best part, and Tennille had sewed on about a million of them—even though she hated sewing. Good for her.

"Now, remember," I said to the assembled group of sweaty little bouncy athletes. "if you're one of our white costume group, it's because we trust you the most not to spill anything on it. Don't violate our trust, okay, kids? We're counting on these to stay sparkling clean from now to the end of the performance."

A bunch of moms nodded their assent.

"You're going to be great, especially on the 'Here Comes Santa Claus' routine. You guys are getting that one nearly perfect already."

One little girl with pigtails—Isla, I think her name was—raised her hand. "We're dedicating this show to you, Miss Danica." She smiled. "We are so glad you can remember us again."

"Thanks, everyone." I placed a hand on my heart. "You're wonderful. It's great to be with you again. I really missed you."

Probably. Not that I could recall any emotion I'd experienced during the black hole of my missing two months. "Let's make it a great show."

"But, Miss Danica?" Isla interjected. "Don't *you* do any gymnastics demonstrations yet, okay?"

"You got it." I gave her the thumbs up.

The kids and parents left, and Tennille sidled up to me. "How long until you can resume your workouts? Are you even going to?"

Good question. "I have an appointment with—I guess he's my neurologist, since I saw his name on a sheet of paper on my desk—Dr. Chen next month. Until then, I'm playing it safe."

"Good. If it were up to me, I'd consider selling the place, after a wreck like that."

Truthfully, the back of my head still hurt. But something told me I'd hit the area near my forehead when I flew from the uneven bars. "Tennille, can you reenact my accident?"

"And hit my head and turn into a whole different person for who knows how long? No, thanks."

"I mean verbally." Sheesh.

She described it to me, and sure enough, according to Tennille, who'd been eyewitness to the scene of the disaster, I'd hit my forehead. A bump the size of a plum, for good measure. The back of my head would have nothing to do with that, unless it was some kind of percussive thing, slowly working its way around to the back of my head. The top and front didn't hurt at all anymore. I rubbed the tender area back there gently.

Nope. Still hurt. *Why?*

We put away the trampolines and prepped heavier mats for the older class, which would be showing up any minute to practice their "Jingle Bell Rock" routine. Then, we stopped beside the water cooler.

"When you looked through your photos on your phone from the last several weeks, did that, by chance, give you any clues to your mysterious connection to Jeremy Houston?"

A gasp escaped my throat. It was so obvious! Why hadn't I

thought of it? "I haven't looked through them."

"Friend. You really do need help from the neurologist. You're not thinking straight. Do you want me to go with you to your appointment with Dr. Chen? Or should we see if they have an opening for an emergency patient right now?"

I pushed her shoulder. "I'm fine. But you're right. I should look through those photos." But not right now. Not until I was somewhere safe. Somewhere I could scream into a pillow if needed.

That night, I found some leftovers in my fridge. Pasta with some kind of cream sauce—delicious. Curl-my-toes and make me sigh like a satisfied woman delicious. If only there were more in another Tupperware somewhere. But alas. However, I did locate a strawberry thing with cream cheese and pretzels that just about leveled me. How did someone mortal make this? It was incredible.

Instead of looking at my photos on my phone like a smart person, I started digging through the kitchen drawers, in case the Cooking Genius had left evidence or recipes or clues.

Nada.

I examined the contents of the fridge, calculating that I had enough amazing leftovers in there to last me about four more meals, but after that, I was back to burnt toast.

This was not acceptable, not after what I'd tasted today. Once a woman had bathed her taste buds in such decadence, how could she return to the scraps and crumbs of her normal life?

From another mystery container, I spooned up a delicious soup. *Chicken broth, white beans, a touch of curry.* Wait a cotton-picking minute. I now had palate skills and could discern ingredients in delicious soups? No way.

I gobbled the rest of the soup, guessing garlic, onion, a hint of dried mustard, and some sliced green onion were involved in this recipe.

Was there hope for me? Was I a chef in embryo and didn't know it? Now, *now* I had real incentive to check out my phone's camera storage—on the off-chance I'd taken photos of recipes or of myself at the stove wearing an apron, for proof that I was involved in the making of these incredible gastronomic inventions.

Settling down on the sofa, I placed a pillow on my lap—in case of scream needs—and opened my photos app.

My corneas melted. I swear, they seared right off. I'd never see again.

First photo. *Jeremy?*

Next photo. *Jeremy Houston and me?*

It went on. *Jeremy smiling.*

Me, smiling while Jeremy and I hugged—closely. Like he owned me. Or vice versa. Like I wanted to own him.

I scrolled faster. All of the pictures looked like they were happening in a parallel universe. This had to be my evil twin, Bizarro Danica, who'd taken over my life and kept me drugged in a basement while she did terrible things with my name and reputation. Argh!

Photos, photos, all with Jeremy.

Finally, cooking pictures. *Jeremy at the stove.*

Me at the stove, wearing a man's shirt—that looked like the one Jeremy had been wearing in the previous photo.

I choked on the back of my tongue. Me, in Jeremy's shirt? Say it wasn't so! I wasn't wearing Jeremy's clothes because I'd … No! I wasn't that kind of girl. I was a good girl. With morals. A girl who not only didn't sleep with Jeremy Houston, one who didn't sleep around at all. One who was saving that part of life for the Real Deal. The big M-word.

The hyperventilation resurged. I shoved my phone between the couch cushions and ran for the back door. Even autumn air couldn't stop these dramatic gulps of horror. *No, please say I'm not living that life!*

How could I be sure? No way was I contacting Jeremy Houston. Never. Not a chance in heck. Even if I did and if I asked him point blank whether … *anything* had happened between us, what incentive would a guy like that have to tell me the truth? I'd never be able to trust his answer, one way or another.

Oh, this was the most ridiculous thing that had ever happened to me in my life. Beyond it. More than if I'd lost my mind, sold the gym, and moved to the city.

My head pounded. I went back inside, grabbed my purse, and then locked up my house and headed to my car for a drive. To my mother's house.

I know! Brainstorm! I got my best ideas while driving. *I'll book an appointment with a gynecologist. She can tell whether I've ... you know.*

I couldn't even *think* the term, for the horror of it. Surely I hadn't betrayed myself to that degree while I was suffering. *But if Jeremy Houston compromised me while I was in a compromised state, I'd compromise him right into his grave.*

Okay, killing him would be extreme, but there would be consequences. I'd think of some punishment that fit the crime. Prison time, shame-fame, public scorning, a big payout from a lawsuit.

No, I couldn't go to Mom's. According to Tennille, I wasn't even allowed to drive yet, post-accident. Sitting in my car, like a fool, I pulled out my phone again.

More, more, more photos. Even one selfie-video at the rec center of me wrapped around him, wearing my tennis skirt as we spun.

I looked happy, elated even. *In love.* Jeremy just looked semi-bored mixed with bewildered. Not besotted. Not even particularly pleased.

What twist had taken place in the space-time continuum to make Jeremy look at me that way? Disinterested. Uninvolved. Not in love with me.

Jeremy had always looked in love with me before.

My head throbbed again. I didn't want to examine it too closely, but I'd known for ages that Jeremy had a thing for me. Always, in fact. I'd brushed it off. He was Jeremy Houston. Goof-off. Class bozo. I'd indulged it, hadn't encouraged it, but I'd never been cruel, never told him to buzz off. In fact, I'd defended him when my parents and sister had gossiped about that shirtless, painted-blue thing at the football game.

Well, until Angelica's wedding when the jerk decided to prank our family and took it too far, that was.

Pranks. Argh, but I hated pranks. So much. And pranksters by correlation. The moment Jeremy had crossed from the clown act to get everyone's attention into play-tricks-on-people-to-make-them-look-bad territory, I'd washed my hands of him. Instantly.

You don't just go and pull a prank on my older sister's wedding. Not when a prank is what had caused her life's biggest pain in the first place.

Enough of this. Enough of *all* of this. Whatever had happened while I was brainless, I didn't need it now. I swiped through the pictures, deleting them all as I went.

Well, except the one of the meal with the chicken and the layered ice cream dessert. I needed that one for reference. But the others went straight to the trash. Where they belonged.

Like Jeremy Houston himself.

Oh, and there was another one with food. What was that, fish? That was *me*, cleaning a fish. A rainbow trout! What, really? I'd cleaned a fish? I loved fish. Loved fishing. Was there any way I'd caught it? And then, there in the pan, the fish sizzled, covered in a flour dusting. Mmm. The skin probably got crispy and the meat probably was flaky and divine, and ...

Um, that was a photo of my arms—I could tell from that constellation of freckles near the wrist—turning the fish in the pan. Wait, wait, wait. I'd cooked something? Something *good?*

Flip, flip, flip. I looked back through the ones I'd furiously deleted to find any other cooking shots. Sure enough, interspersed, there were several of food—with hints of my involvement in its preparation. A hand here, a sweater or t-shirt in the background there.

I can cook?

I flopped back against the driver's seat. This went beyond unbelievable. Like Tennille said, I was Drive-Through Danica, cooker of nothing. My mom didn't like cooking, was never taught to cook, was too busy being Angelica's caregiver to learn or to teach me. I just had no fundamentals. Oh, but I had always wished I could cook.

Had Jeremy Houston taught me to cook?

Chapter 3

"Thank you for working me in early, before my original appointment." I knotted a Kleenex in my hands while I sat in the plush chair and talked to Dr. Chen in his office the Monday after Thanksgiving. "So, you *have* heard of someone losing their memories a second time? After they come out of the first bout of memory loss?"

Dr. Chen looked over his glasses at me, steepling his fingers. "The brain is a mystery. We understand only so much about how it functions. But, yes. Selective memory loss, *post*-memory loss, has been known to occur."

The vocabulary of it was dizzying. I tugged at the Kleenex so hard it fragmented, little fibers and dust motes floating onto my black trousers.

"But is this a new amnesia, or is it the same one?" Basically, I wanted to ask what to expect. "Is it possible that during my memory loss period, I had a … personality shift?"

"What do you mean by that? Please don't be quite so concerned about the fact you'd forgotten your third-grandmother's name. Candalaria, it's an unusual name, to be sure." Dr. Chen and I had discussed this fact first. "Forgetting a name is quite normal, even without an injury."

True, but I meant something more like, "Would I have forsaken my core values?" My heart palpitated. "I have some photos of myself doing uncharacteristic things during that time."

Dr. Chen raised a brow. "Jumping out of a plane-type photos, or like robbing a bank-type photos? Or …"

"Cooking."

Now both his brows rose. "I see."

"To actually see, you have to know that I don't cook. The world at large knows this. It's one of those immutable facts like gravity or the multiplication tables. But in the pictures, doctor, I cooked meals. *Meals*." And I'd kissed Jeremy Houston. I prayed nothing beyond that.

"That's not unusual." He scrawled something on a legal pad. It was probably a doodle of my face with the word *crazy* next to it in block letters and arrows pointing at my head. "What you should know is that many of the struggles we have in life are the result of the limitations we place on ourselves based on our thoughts."

"I used to tell myself I could toast bread without burning it. It never worked. I've tried all that mindset stuff, believe me."

"Not all of it, apparently. And I'm happy for you. You've got some tangible evidence that you can now point to, proving that life the way you see it now isn't the only way it could be. You can expand your vision for yourself. What a gift. Not a lot of people get that in life." He reached over and patted the air near me. "Accept the gift you've been given. Accept that if you tried a new sport or learned a new skill or didn't burn toast in your Amnesia Episode of life, it proves you can do anything you set your mind to. Even make a new friend." He gave a knowing smile.

Ugh. Even Dr. Chen had heard about me and Jeremy Houston, apparently. I darted a glance at the wall, and there hung a plaque declaring him a golf champion at the Wilder River country club.

"I've forgiven you for overextending your return time for the golf cart the other day. You and your companion, I was told, needed it very much for your … activity."

If only someone would saw a hole in the floor in a big circle around my chair and let me fall through it. "I honestly don't have any recollection of that."

"More's the pity." Dr. Chen reassured me that I was normal, gave me hope that I'd eventually be able to recall the events that happened over the past two months, and then ushered me out of his office.

"Not even a CT scan for my time?"

"The nursing staff will schedule that for later in the month, as originally planned."

Oh, right. I'd come in a week early, based on my freak-out.

Outside in the gathering snow, I waited for Mom to drive up. Until the CT scan, I wouldn't be cleared to drive. Which was fine. The way things had been going, I might lose or gain memories any second—so, could I lose the ability to drive a car any second, too? Who knew! No way was I endangering others' lives by driving yet. Even though it required humbling myself and asking for rides.

From my mom.

The back seat of Mom's sedan was filled to the brim with groceries. Wow, she was going all-out for holiday cooking!

"Well, dear. How's Dr. Chen doing?"

"He seemed fine. He's a good golfer. He might like a nice golf glove for Christmas."

"You're always thinking about what people might like. Even now." Mom beamed at me while we waited at the stoplight. "After everything you've been through."

"I learned from the best." I patted her arm. "What's with all the shopping? Are you inviting the whole neighborhood?"

"Well, you seemed so interested in cooking lately. The last few times I've talked to you, it's been recipe, recipe, recipe, ingredients, ingredients, ingredients. Is your new boyfriend a chef? We could have him help cook Christmas dinner. Brine the turkey, maybe. I was disappointed you didn't invite him for Thanksgiving, to be honest, but I didn't want to bring it up on the holiday itself."

Bless her for that, and for tiptoeing around me, but I needed to set her straight. "I don't have a new boyfriend." If I had to endure this conversation with Mom, it'd be a long sixty miles back to Wilder River.

"Oh." Mom's face fell. "I thought—"

"There might have been some confusion for a while, but that's all been straightened out. I'm not seeing anyone, and no one will be joining us for Christmas."

"Then how about finally taking an interest in that nice young man from the plant?"

Not this again. Every mother of a single daughter in town laid awake nights scheming on how her daughter could catch the eye of Garrett Bolton.

"He's successful, friendly, well-respected, takes good care of his mother—without living in her basement. All green flags, as far as I can see."

Yeah, but he was also Jeremy Houston's cousin. That was the only red flag I needed.

"And he's athletic. Do you remember when he threw that wonderful touchdown pass during your last home football game during your senior year? I'm sure he'd be interested if you'd pay him some attention. You're quite a catch yourself."

"Mom, how is Angelica?"

"You're changing the subject."

Yeah, to the topic that was always a surefire exit from whatever I didn't want to talk about, especially Garrett Bolton. "When is her surgery? I want to go down and stay with her for that."

"It's the same day as the Christmas showcase for the gymnastics class."

"What? No!" Since when were surgeries scheduled for Saturdays? "I need to be there with her."

"She has her husband. She has her mother." Mom patted my arm with a soothing touch.

"Wait. You're going?"

"No, but …"

See? That's what I thought. "She'll heal so much faster if I'm there, Mom. I can do all the cooking, the cleaning, the fetching, the pill-counting."

"The cooking?" Mom raised a brow and snorted a short laugh. "All she needs is her husband. Their wedding wasn't yesterday. He knows how to care for her."

"Is he taking off work?" Alarm rose in me, pitching higher and higher.

"I'm sure he is."

But she didn't *know* that. She hadn't *verified.* I could only hear a dull squeal going off in my head. "I'm calling Tennille and asking her to handle the showcase. She's been doing everything herself all this time since my accident. She can manage one showcase."

"Honey, the day-to-day is one thing. The showcase is another."

"Mom, this is Angelica's surgery. Her big chance to walk normally for the first time since she was six years old." Since that *I won't use the term in polite company and I am polite company so I won't use it even in my head* of a prankster spread cooking oil on the balance beam at Angelica's gymnastics class, and she'd fallen onto her leg with such a twisting break to both femur and hip, including a puncture wound, that the doctors feared she wouldn't live.

All the bleeding.

She'd lived, but she never walked well, and she certainly never got to live out her childhood dream of becoming a gymnast.

I had only been a small child at the time, and the family barely whispered about it, but over the years, I'd pieced together the details.

And I'd dedicated myself to gymnastics—by proxy.

And I hated pranksters. Forever.

"I'm going to Reedsville. And I'm taking care of her."

Mom watched while I stomped up to my front door. While I was at the stoop putting the key in the lock, she rolled down her window and called to me, "Don't you want these groceries? Are you giving up on your cooking dream?"

"Take them to Starlight Haven, the women's shelter." One of them probably knew how to cook.

Not me.

Despite the snow, I rode my bicycle downtown to the gym. My mountain bike tires had pretty good tread. I'd have to tell Tennille as soon as possible that I'd miss the Christmas showcase, and I needed to tell her face-to-face. She'd understand. It was for Angelica!

Yet, when I arrived, bad luck. No Tennille. One of the assistant teachers had the seven-to-nine-year-old class well in hand. I walked out back to the employee parking lot to check for Tennille's car.

A dark form moved in the snow-capped bushes at the far edge of the lot. My spine tingled.

"Who's there?" I called. "No one is allowed back here. This business property is a designated safe space for children. If you don't come out and identify yourself immediately, I'm morally obligated to call the police."

Nothing. I waited a long time. Still nothing. And no Tennille.

I went back inside and put on some Christmas music to try to calm my nerves, but a few minutes later, I went to the back door again—just to be certain.

Instead of a creepy creepster in the parking lot, there was a huge bouquet of flowers in a crystal vase. I stooped and picked it up. It had to weigh ten pounds, if not more. Either the vase was lead crystal, or I was weak, or ... Ooh, there was a card.

Because you missed the flowers of fall.

I held the vase out, looking more carefully at the bouquet.

Wow. Every single one was a quintessential autumn-time flower: deep red chrysanthemums, huge sunflowers, purple dahlia, cone flower, yellow and red roses. How amazingly sweet of someone to ...

Wait a second. Who had left this? And was it for me?

"Tennille?" I marched the bouquet into the gym, where Tennille was near the front desk, shrugging out of her denim jacket. "Did your husband send these?"

"Liam doesn't believe in cut flowers."

Seriously? "Does he not understand women?"

"Oh, he's all right. It's just he holds this odd belief that cut flowers are a symbol of death, and he'd rather plant me a rosebush or a flowering tree or whatever. No roses in a vase from Liam. They must be for you. Who's sending you flowers?"

"Someone who knows I missed the autumn blooms." And who understood what that meant for me, since I adored fall. "It's sweet, but also ..."

"It's obviously from Jeremy Houston."

"Jeremy Houston could never afford a vase of flowers this size. He went off and joined the army. He's probably on infantry pay. They'd never promote anyone like him."

Tennille rested on the counter and put her chin on her hands, batting her eyes. "Unless they saw him in his uniform and the commanding officers were all women."

"He's not *that* attractive." It was a good thing that my body hadn't been possessed by Pinocchio while I was temporarily insane, or he and I would be having nose problems right now. Jeremy Houston—according to my photographic evidence—was incredibly attractive. Like, melt-my-inhibitions gorgeous.

"Well, he's also not that broke, either." Tennille pushed off the counter and moved to take some files from a stack near the phone. "I heard from someone who heard from someone else that he got out of the army and became a businessman, and that his business in the city is doing really well."

"Is he a drug dealer, or something?" People who called themselves *businessmen* in enigmatic terms like that were rarely doing something aboveboard. "Or worse? Is he an attorney defending drug dealers?"

"Real estate. Commercial properties brokering, to be specific." She whipped out her phone. "You know, we should just verify."

Oh, no. I was not going to stoop to the level of doing an internet search on the guy. My shoulders bunched up at the idea. "Stop it,

Tennille. He's not an object."

"So, you do admit to objectifying him." She gave a playful grin. "Oh, fine." She put away her phone. "I'll just wait until curiosity burns you up—once I've told you I heard he made a nine-figure profit on a deal in September before he disappeared from the real estate landscape in Reedsville. We here in Wilder River know where he was, but the rest of the world was missing him. *Is* missing him, I should say."

Every single factoid from her mouth was like a round of gunfire from an automatic weapon. They pierced me one by one, sinking deep into me, painful, each bit something I desperately wanted to reject.

"You've got to be mistaken. This is Jeremy Houston we're talking about. The guy couldn't hold down a minimum wage job, let alone manage big negotiations like that. It's got to be a mix-up. There has to be another Jeremy Houston." It wasn't a completely uncommon name.

Pinocchio, eat your heart out.

"Uh-huh." Tennille sauntered off to help the assistant coach start the next class.

I still hadn't given her the bad news about my upcoming trip to Reedsville to be with Angelica. I waited until she'd done what she needed to, and when she came back to the desk, I launched.

"Can you handle the Christmas showcase alone?"

"Alone!"

"It's scheduled for the same day as Angelica's surgery."

"And?"

"And she needs help."

"She's married. Her husband will help. That's a weekend. He won't have to work."

"Brady wouldn't know the first thing about how to care for her post-operation."

"And you would? You're not a nurse, Danica."

"No, but I play one on TV." She didn't take my joke well. "Fine, but I was in the hospital recently *receiving* care." Not that I could remember a single day of that. "And I've got an instinct for how to help people."

"You can help them most by letting Brady rise to the occasion."

Humph. Everyone was ganging up on me. "I'm going."

Tennille's face filled with thunder. "I'll handle the Christmas showcase." She marched off. I thought I heard her mutter something about *business partners pulling their weight or regretting it.*

I was left with the giant vase of flowers and a semi-yucky feeling.

Tennille had been right—they must be a gift from Jeremy Houston. Jeremy had probably been the lurker making rustling sounds in the bushes behind the gymnastics building a few minutes ago. Hmm. I could call the police on him, but I stopped myself.

For one thing, Jeremy had kept a respectful distance. For another, the police might request the flowers as evidence.

The flowers were too gorgeous to be wasted by being placed in an evidence room.

I leaned in and inhaled their fragrance. Mmm. So nice. I did love autumn flowers. The bouquet had multiple types. I recognized the main varieties—roses, mums, sunflowers, but others I had to look up: asters, Russian sage, cimicifuga, sedum, rudbeckia, and phlox. Jeremy—for all his glaringly obvious faults—did have great taste in flowers.

Chapter 4

T he date of my originally scheduled appointment with Dr. Chen approached. I called to see whether I was still on the schedule, considering I'd wedged in that bonus appointment during my initial freak-out. They confirmed, and I went in for my CT scan. My results wouldn't be in for a while, but I kept my appointment.

"Are you feeling any better?" he asked, still doodling on that legal pad. "Any recollections for the episode between?"

"Is that what we're calling it now?" I'd been calling it The Black Hole. But *Episode Between* worked.

"It's a nice turn of phrase, right?" He beamed, clearly proud of himself. "So? Have you come to terms with it?"

"Terms? No." The unsettling feeling that I'd lived a foreign life only surged harder, every passing day. Seeing the flowers on the countertop in my kitchen didn't help matters. Luckily, as Tennille's husband Liam would say, they'd die soon, and there was that. "As long as I'm missing those months, I'm going to feel off-balance. Like a stranger took over. Honestly, Dr. Chen, in my *real* state of mind, I never would have given Jeremy Houston the time of day, let alone overextended the rental on a golf cart with him." Et cetera, et cetera.

"From what I hear, Jeremy Houston is extremely well respected in commercial real estate brokerage circles. My second cousin is a wildly successful businesswoman who lives in Reedsville, and she's looking to buy a commercial property to diversify. She's been waiting weeks for Jeremy to resurface in the real estate business world so she can work with him. You might want to give him another chance."

"If you knew how many chances I'd given him in the past, you'd never tell me that, Dr. Chen." I brushed dust particles off my lap. Enough was enough of this conversation. "Can you just call me when the CT scan results come in?"

That was it. I had a brain tumor! That was the explanation.

"Sure." He stood with me and walked me to the door of his office. "And Danica? If you really do want some of those memories back, I suggest you try reenacting some of the activities you know you participated in—with the people who were there—while you experienced the Between Episode."

There was that term again, but reversed. "Thank you, doctor, but I'm not getting together with Jeremy Houston for anything."

I left.

On the ride home, with Mom chatting about Christmas shopping she'd done while I was in the appointment, I conceded mentally that Dr. Chen had a fair point. "Hey, Mom, what did you end up doing with all those groceries you bought last week?"

"Most of them are still in the garage, since I haven't had a chance to drive out to Starlight Haven yet. A few of the fresh items are in my refrigerator. Are you hungry? Are you ... low on funds? You haven't worked regularly in months, and I'm sure there are medical bills piling up."

Oh, dear. Were there? I'd barely thought of getting the mail. Owning a gymnastics business didn't do much for health insurance benefits. I had some simple coverage, but ... man. This could get serious fast.

"Can I have some of the groceries? I think I will actually try again to cook. I found some pictures of recipes I want to try to make."

"Oh, honey. Are you sure?" Mom looked both hopeful and scared as she changed routes toward her house instead of mine.

I was sure. We collected the items—a really good variety representing the four food groups—and headed to my house. There were a lot. Mom helped me take them inside, and we put them in the pantry and fridge.

Then, I pulled open the freezer and showed her the cake. "Once I've figured out a couple of meals, I'm going to try to make this again."

"You made that?"

Probably. I thought so. "Do you want a slice?" I got out a plate for her and gave her a piece. "It's been in the freezer, but—"

"But nothing!" Mom said through her chewing. "It's incredible. Use all those groceries. Make more of this ice cream cake, though, and bring some to me, okay?"

Instead, I sent the remainder of the cake home with her. She and Dad could finish it faster than I could on my own. Besides, I had loads of food now—which was the same as loads of hope. Hope for a better world with good cooking in it.

Or not.

Six hours later, mashed potato clumps decorated my ceiling, thanks to an unfortunate hand-mixer slip, a whole three-pound bag of carrots had gone from caramelized to carbonized, and my smoke alarm had gone off five times.

But I pressed on. Luckily, there were YouTube channels for this type of thing, and I paused, rewound, and rewatched segments until I got a skill right.

The flowers from the vase kind of smiled at me from the dining room. Not sure if it was a mocking or approving smile.

Or if I was going crazy to think that bouquets of flowers could smile.

Yes. To all of that.

Finally, I had a plateful of delicious-looking food. I set the table with a cloth napkin and a goblet of ice water, and I lit a candle on the table. Candles made everything more special. *Where did that phrase come from?* It felt hauntingly familiar, and not like something I'd say myself.

I lowered my eyes and touched my palms together.

"For what I am about to eat, may the Lord make me truly grateful." If my cooking skills couldn't create something edible, maybe God could change it into something that was. That's what I really meant by that prayer.

With a steeling breath, I took my fork, stabbed a bite of meatloaf, a caramelized carrot (from round two), and lifted them to my mouth.

Nope.

Nope, nope, nope.

I spit the mostly raw meat into my napkin, and took a big drink of water to swish out the acrid residue from the burnt—not caramelized like I'd told myself—carrots.

Even God couldn't make my cooking taste good.

I dumped it in the trash and called for delivery from the pizza shop. They knew *Drive-through Danica* by voice—and exactly what I'd order. It was there at their drive-up window in twenty minutes. And I was a few dollars poorer.

I really should learn this cooking thing. It'd be good for my wallet, as well as my psyche, not to mention my overall health.

Sigh. It was time to face facts. *I might need Jeremy Houston to teach me.*

No! I wasn't going to reach out to him. I probably didn't even have his number, and I wouldn't contact him if I did. Not an option. Instead, I looked through the photos from the trash bin on my phone. Maybe there were cooking hints in them I could decipher, since YouTube had obviously failed me.

I flipped through them again, this time less horrified, so I could take them in a little better—since I was resigned to the fact I'd lived a life of sheer stupidity for two months' time. Whatever. Everyone makes mistakes. Few people had as solid an excuse as I did for their lapses in judgment. I'd had an *Episode Between.*

Scroll, scroll, scroll. Hey, what was that series of dark photos? I adjusted the settings on my phone to examine them better. Huh, there was the river—and some chairs and poles, and just a second! Had Jeremy taken me fishing?

I love fishing! I hadn't been fishing in years, not since my cousin Veronica and I went every night for a summer when we were kids. Wow. I rubbed my forehead. The sight of the river in the pictures, though obscured by lack of lighting, spread calmness inside me. I could almost hear its slow current, feel the cold breeze coming off the water, smell the dry grasses of fall.

Jeremy Houston had taken me fishing at the river before it snowed.

And he'd taught me to cook.

And he'd noticed I'd missed the autumn's flowers.

None of those actions resembled pranks.

Maybe I can see why I might have liked him.

I shut off the photo app and went outside. The large mailbox at the end of my gravel drive beckoned. I went to it and found more mail than anyone should ever receive.

The rest of that night was spent under the weight of sorting mail—and not nearly enough of it was stuff I could automatically junk, like fliers or credit card offers. Way too much of it was medical. And there seemed to be far more business-related mail for the owner of Candy Cane Cottage than usual, and in official-looking envelopes, too.

I tore the largest one open. Out fell a stack of papers so thick and terrifying I let it drop like it was on fire.

Paperwork and I did not coexist well. But something told me I should buckle down and examine it. Party of the first part, me, party of the second part, Tennille Underwood-Lexington. Candy Cane Cottage, its address, hereafter referred to as The Property, blah, blah, blah.

My eyes lurched to a halt. I went back and reread the blah, blah, blah.

Party of the First Part does hereby quitclaim The Property to Party of the Second Part.

At the bottom, there was a line filled in with my signature, as well as the date. Well, not *quite* my signature. It looked shaky. Spindly. Not quite the right capital Ds for Danica or Denton.

Forged? Or had my injured self penned them?

Tennille's was already on the other line, and dated three weeks ago, alongside a witness's signature that I couldn't read.

Three weeks ago? That was while I was still ... not myself.

Just a cotton-picking minute! I was no contracts expert, but to me, this looked like a deal where I had supposedly agreed to sign away full ownership of Candy Cane Cottage—the property and the business—to Tennille, my business partner.

That made no sense!

Unless it was something I'd discussed with Tennille during my fugue state—and had been talked into by someone nefarious, like *Jeremy Houston!*

My blood insta-boiled. I surged to my feet and paced the tile of the room, but that wasn't enough. I added the kitchen to my pacing route, and that still didn't help. Outside, I marched the length of my snow-lined gravel drive all the way to the street and back, but on the second time through, I kept going. Each of my steps could have registered on the Richter scale, I was stomping it out so hard.

Being this upset could cause permanent joint damage to my knees and hips.

It wasn't good to be this upset.

Especially without knowing what had caused the situation. Finally, when I could breathe better and control the vibrato of anger in my voice, I called up Tennille. In my sweetest, calmest tone I asked, "You said you sent me some paperwork, right?"

"I thought maybe you hadn't seen it yet."

"It's for real, then?"

"Sure. The lawyers hammered it out perfectly."

"Lawyers." Plural. Tennille was one of the few people who'd known the whole sequence of my memory losses. "Did anyone advise me about it?" I had to ask.

"Sure. We went through everything, and you okayed it with someone you trusted, and—you don't remember?"

She *knew* I didn't remember. My neck grew hot, and I pulled at the collar of my turtleneck sweater. "Refresh my memory."

"Come on, Danica. It's late. I'm with Liam. We haven't had a date night in weeks, since you left me the full brunt of responsibility of Candy Cane Cottage—business and upkeep and all those kids and the employees. Come on. Call me back later."

She hung up.

But I was still hung up on the paperwork. *You went through it with someone you trusted.* If it had happened during my Between Episode— why was I using that annoying phrase right now—that could likely mean only one person.

I scrolled through my contacts and dialed the number listed for Jeremy Houston.

Chapter 5

J eremy Houston did not pick up. An automated response declared that his voice mail was also full. I tried a text, and an auto-responder said he was out of the office until further notice.

Well, that was unexpected.

What had I assumed? That Jeremy Houston had been standing somewhere, breathless, on pins and needles, waiting for my call? That he spent all his days loitering in florist shops and snowy parking lots, pining for me?

The next morning, my ire had not abated. I tried calling Tennille, but she didn't answer. It was her morning to work as a jiu-jitsu instructor. I probably should have remembered that. But even when class time ended, she still didn't respond.

I peered at the paperwork again. In the morning's clear light, it appeared even worse. Not only did this contract seem to transfer ownership of the gymnastics business to Tennille and Liam, it included something called a quitclaim deed to the property itself.

But! That building had belonged to my great-great-great-grandmother, Candalaria Merchant. Inspired by her late husband's last name, she'd opened a shop, the first ever hard-goods store in Wilder River when it was first settled. With grit and persistence, she'd run her business, ordered and shipped in lumber and nails, and more or less facilitated the building up of the town out of the wilderness. I'd been named for her, Danica Candalaria Denton.

And I'd bought the run-down, unimproved building that had housed her store when it came up for auction, as the first thing I'd done when I graduated from college. Putting a gym there had been the only thought in my mind. Three goals—honoring Great-Grandma Candalaria, living out Angelica's dream, and running my own business—had all converged in Candy Cane Cottage, which I'd named in honor of Grandma Candy, not caring the title sounded nothing like a gymnastics spot. It was the type of name that appealed to kids, made them want to go to training, and that was what had mattered. As did Grandma and my connection to her.

There was no way—in any rational state of mind—I would have signed that contract.

And Tennille knew that.

The names associated with the law firm were listed at the top of the contract, and I stared at them hard. They seemed familiar. In spite of my ethical stand against searching people on the internet, I looked up the lawyers, one by one.

Sure enough, one hailed from Wilder River—Ivan Rutledge. I scrolled down to see his picture at the bottom of his bio.

He couldn't look more like Liam Lexington if he'd gotten one of those major plastic surgeries. Whoa. Like, identical twins. Had to be one of Liam's relatives.

I shut off the computer, my stomach churning way too much for this early in the morning.

Who could help me?

My parents were not worldly, not business people. Mom always took care of Angelica. Dad was a retired high school band teacher, with a personality the antithesis of shrewd negotiator. All smiles and open book.

Angelica was brilliant—but at chemistry, not contracts. Her husband was an accountant, great with numbers but not as great with people, which was why I was insisting on going to be with Angelica after her surgery.

A growl tore from my lungs. I had no one—*no one*—in my life who could help me with this.

Jeremy Houston, my gut whispered.

Jeremy was not answering his phone. So, my gut was useless, too.

I marched to the cupboard and shushed my useless gut with my go-to comfort food: a brownie, the kind from cellophane with rainbow sprinkles. But that only kept it busy for a couple of minutes, and it came back—this time in a stern voice, telling me that Jeremy Houston had a good reputation. And he'd sent me flowers *after* I'd violently ejected him from my home.

No, he hadn't accepted my call. But could I find him somewhere?

"Mom?" I asked when she picked up her phone. "Can you get me the number for Garrett Bolton?"

A squeal of delight that could have broken glass shrilled through the receiver on my phone. "You're calling him? Oh, sugar. I'm so happy that you're being courageous."

"Courageous." Right. "Thanks," I said when she promised to get *right back* to me.

A few minutes later, I had Garrett's number in hand. But how to proceed? I texted him and asked him to see whether Jeremy Houston was around and if he could ask Jeremy to get in touch with me. It was an emergency.

Thirty minutes later, there was a knock on my door.

"Mom, you didn't have to come over just because—" Instead of finding Mom standing there with another bag of groceries, the sight of Jeremy Houston slammed me.

Taller, wider in the shoulders than I ever would have expected him to become, and with a muscle-twitch in a chiseled jaw, he filled the whole doorway. If what everyone said was true and he'd gone into the military, man, he would have looked *fine* in a uniform. My eyes lingered too long on that broad chest.

Jeremy gave me one of those *I'm here, now what* looks, challenging me, as if daring me to cross him.

Or maybe I was misreading.

Whatever his look, intensity thudded in the air between us, and a ghost of a memory—a remnant of something that might have happened in a parallel life—swished through my mind ever so swiftly. A single pulse of true connection.

And then it was gone, leaving me desperate to reclaim it.

I brushed it aside. *I can't be feeling that.* Instead, I mentally reverted to the contract. "You have a lot of nerve."

"You've said that in the past." His gaze was hard. "So why summon me? Just to rip me to shreds? Wouldn't that be more satisfying if you did it publicly?"

"Jeremy." I huffed in frustration. "Did you encourage me to sign this document?" I went over to the table and brought it to him.

"Rules of propriety dictate that you should invite me in."

Glugh. "Fine. Come in. But not if you're planning to accost me in any way."

"You're safe." His words sizzled in my ears, a déjà vu of the most unsettling kind. "Now, what is this paperwork?"

Jeremy followed me into the living room—the scene of his former crime. He gave a quick glance at my Christmas tree, which had lights but no decorations yet. His flowers sat on the front room coffee table, having held up amazingly well for over a week. I'd only needed to remove a couple of crumpled blooms so far. He eyed them briefly but said nothing. My face flushed hot, revealing my totally mixed-up emotions.

I took a fortifying breath against all those pheromones detonating my will power and said, "Tennille mailed me this. Apparently, I signed something that gives her and her husband my entire business." Hearing the facts aloud was like a cheese grater against my eardrum. "Dr. Chen said I will eventually be able to remember everything that happened between the time of my original accident and the time I regained my memory." Not exactly true, but I decided to speak it as an act of faith. "However, I can't *imagine* a scenario where I would have been persuaded"—I speared him with a look—"to sign away my life's work."

"And? Why are you asking me?"

"Because *apparently* while I was in a compromised state, someone took advantage of me." I raised a brow. He knew what I was thinking of—his eyes slid toward the floor where I'd been lying the last time I saw him. "And you seem like the likely culprit."

Culprit. There. I liked that word. I folded my arms over my chest as if to underscore it.

"Danica, I didn't do anything inappropriate, either *with* you or *to* you." His voice was firm, as if he were biting down on a leather strap while he spoke.

"Why was I wearing *your shirt* in a photograph, then?"

"Grease spattered on your own clothes while you were making homemade doughnuts, and you said it was a fire hazard. I had an extra in my truck. It was long enough that it hid your shorts." His jaw worked. "Geez, Danica. I'm not that guy. I respect women. I respect you."

The declaration resonated in the air between us, and I stared at him, gauging his sincerity while his words sank into my mind. *He didn't do anything inappropriate with or to me.*

That photo of me in the man's shirt, then, didn't mean anything terrible had gone awry with my moral standards. A whoosh of relief left my lungs. "Thank you."

My gaze met his, which was still edgy and stern. It disarmed me, put me on the defensive all of a sudden. "Look, I'm sorry for assuming the worst. It's just that these photos in my phone showed ..." I shook my head. "Yeah. Well, what about this contract?" I jabbed the paperwork he held with my fingertip. "Why did you encourage me to agree to sign it? I ask because according to the photographic history on my camera, you seemed to have been a constant presence in my life while I was"—how to put it?—"incapacitated. And they tell me you're a businessman. So I would have consulted with you."

"No," was all he said. He flipped to the back page. "Who are these people?" He peered at the names of the lawyers listed in the letterhead. "Have you and Tennille ever discussed anything of this type? To your knowledge, I mean?"

"There's the salient phrase: *to your knowledge.* Honestly, Jeremy, very little in life has been reliably *to my knowledge* lately. Big gaps of reality are missing." My eyes darted to his lips, which I'd apparently kissed on multiple occasions—without my knowledge.

How would they feel on mine in this reality? I pressed my hand to my cheek, willing myself not to slap it. He was Jeremy Houston, Certified Buffoon. My life was too jammed with reality for sidetrack fantasies where I wasted time with someone as crackpot and careless as Jeremy Houston. A prankster. Who'd ruined Angelica's wedding.

"With your permission, I'll send this to Mark."

"Who's Mark?"

"I forgot." He grimaced, a look that communicated *you forgot* instead. "My attorney in Reedsville. He looked at some medical forms for you in the past. He's aware of your situation."

He was? An attorney in the city knew about my amnesia? How humiliating. "Why would he be interested in my medical documents?"

"Oh, just a little matter of rights the hospital network had tried to get you to sign away. Mark helped them see the error in the verbiage of the contract, and they quickly corrected it."

My heart began to pound erratically—a bunny rabbit hopping among drunk grasshoppers. "Really?" A warm cloak of protection wrapped around me. *Jeremy arranged that? For me?* "What are the details of that?"

He filled my eardrums with legal jargon that bounced right off, but which left me with the simple impression that indeed, he'd been looking out for me, and that his attorney had had my best interests in mind.

"Thanks." What else could I say? I dropped some of my shields.

This version of Jeremy Houston sitting beside me didn't have the air of a prankster at this point—or of someone who had to prove his worth to anyone. Confidence rolled off him in waves. I couldn't deny that the charisma affected me. "I'd be grateful if you could give this to your friend Mark. What will I owe him?"

Jeremy gave me a withering look that said, *you can't afford Mark.* "I'll take care of it. As a friend."

A friend! Suddenly he'd put me in the friend zone? Or put himself into my friend zone? My body chemistry revolted, begging to be consulted in that definition. I just nodded. "A friend in a time of need, and all that. Thank you."

"You're the one who helps people in need all the time, Danica. Just let yourself be on the receiving end for once." He stood to leave. "Give Mark a day to look it over. It's the weekend. I don't know his schedule. Then call or shoot me a text, and I'll let you know what he came back with."

"You're not going to call me as soon as an answer comes from him?"

He gave a careless raise of his shoulder. "I would, but I have a lot of work I'm trying to catch up on. I've been away from the office for several weeks. But I'll make time for this."

Oh. He really was doing me a favor. And I'd taken him away from his job today. Interrupted his day with some kind of imperious summons, expecting him to ... what? Fall at my feet? Like he had for ages past?

Not this Jeremy Houston. Strong in physicality and in his aura. Everything about him exuded *not the old Jeremy.* With that much confidence, that much swagger, maybe the rumors were true and he really had earned millions of dollars. He sure put off those vibes.

Jeremy left, and I stared after him as he drove away in a very nice truck that looked too high for me to climb into comfortably.

He didn't even look back or wave goodbye.

My stomach did some kind of round-off back handspring, as if to say, *The Jeremy who was here today was a Jeremy Houston I can easily see why I would have fallen for—anytime. Fugue state or not.*

A whole day of waiting for the right time to call him seemed like an eternity.

But it was time to go to Candy Cane Cottage for the all-team rehearsal. Tennille had better be there. And she'd better have some clear answers.

Chapter 6

Tennille didn't show her face that afternoon. I directed the classes in a run-through of the Christmas extravaganza. Of course, I had to defer to the teaching assistant who knew the choreography, but I kept the music running and gave the kids directions for how to enter and exit the "stage," which we had taped out on the mats. They all seemed excited for next weekend's show which we'd do on the actual stage down at the Wilder River recreation center.

"Miss Danica!" A few kids ran up to me. One of them squatted down on the floor and did a backward roll. "That's a winter-pepper."

"A what?" I knelt down to look her in the eye. Her red-sequined costume glittered. "What's a winter-pepper?"

"A backwards somersault!" She broke into giggles and the three kids ran off. Oh, I got it. Somersault, summer-salt, winter-pepper.

"Where's Miss Tennille?" another little girl asked—Shenae, a cute kid with tight curls. "I wanted to show her my band-aid." She held up her finger, wrapped in a pink bandage that was decorated with a cartoon character.

"She couldn't be here today, honey. But I love your band-aid. It's got Princess Cupcake right on it!"

Shenae beamed. "You know about Princess Cupcake?"

Kids were so cute. They often thought adults lived in isolation chambers, unaware of pop culture. "I love how strong she is and how

117

she saves the Candy Kingdom and frees her dad." I'd seen the program just so I could connect with my students, who'd all been talking about the *Candy Kingdom* series of books turned into TV shows for the past two years. "She's brave. Just like you, when you got a cut!"

Shenae grinned, showing a gap for a missing tooth. "I love you, Miss Danica."

"I love you, too." I loved all of them, this job, this gym, this *calling* in life that let me connect the past—my grandmother's and sister's lives—with the present kids taking lessons, and with the future of Wilder River, filled with physically healthy kids full of confidence in their bodies and spirits.

There was no scenario where I would have agreed to sign it away. Not a snowball's chance.

Where is Tennille?

When class ended, I rode my mountain bike to her house. Blast not being able to drive yet! If those CT results would only come in. Geez.

Getting to Tennille and Liam's was no small task. They lived at the top edge of a neighborhood built in the foothills, way up from Peppermint Drop Inn and the other Victorian homes of Wilder River. The houses' styles progressed through the decades as I ascended the hill—from Victorian to arts and crafts. At one point in the mid-century modern homes, I was panting so hard I had to get off my bike and push. Blast my accident! I was stronger than this!

Finally, I made it to their 1970s split-level house—only to find Tennille and Liam hurriedly loading suitcases into the back of a car.

"Going on a trip?" Acidity laced my question. "I got the paperwork in the mail, Liam."

Liam stormed at me. "I told Tennille to tell Ivan not to send you the final copy with the signatures." His teeth were clenched. "I swear, if I ever see that shyster again, I'll"—he made a ring with his hands and shook it, as if choking imaginary Ivan.

Tennille rushed up to me, tears in her eyes. "It's so awful, Danica. I'm so ashamed! When I got your messages this morning, I realized what had happened. That you somehow had copies of the contract. I bet Jeremy's big-shot lawyer in Reedsville wrung them out of Ivan. Ivan and all the Rutledges were always the weak-willed branch of the family."

Rather than explain that Jeremy hadn't brought them to my attention, I said, "Tell me what you were thinking."

"It was so crazy, Danica, when you lost your memory. You didn't know me. You didn't know the kids or the business or anything. You rarely came into work. Yeah, I know the doctors told you you couldn't, but when you showed up, you were useless. I was drowning. I thought if I owned Candy Cane Cottage, I could sell it. Or repurpose it as a jiu-jitsu studio. The kids and I don't really connect, and I am sick to my grave of making costumes." She made a gurgling sound. "Do you know how many calluses my fingertips have from putting sequins on lace? For forty kids?"

"And so you tried to steal my business? And my property?"

"Danica. Don't put it like that."

"What other way is there to put it?" And how had she convinced me to sign that contract? That still seemed so unlikely. "You know the building belonged to my ancestor. You *know* I scrimped and saved to purchase it, to honor her. You know my heart and soul is in it."

"But that's the thing, Danica. *You* didn't know that. When weeks and weeks went by, and you had zero interest in the property or the kids or the business aspect, I got desperate. Liam contacted his cousin Ivan, and we told him what we needed."

"Where was my signature going to come from?"

"You've signed your name a thousand times on paperwork for the shop, Danica. It's not like I don't know exactly what it looks like." She rolled her eyes at my apparent naïveté. "We're partners. We're close."

"That's what I had always thought." And she'd forged my name on the signature line. That fact became painfully obvious. "Forgery is a crime, Tennille."

"Look, there was no guarantee you were *ever* going to remember anything. And you were obviously much more interested in going around town with that multi-millionaire Jeremy Houston, and making out with him in public places. You'd gone off your rocker. I didn't want Candy Cane Cottage to start losing clients—and tank Liam's investment—because of your reputation going down the toilet or because they questioned your mental incompetence. I had to act fast."

All of her excuses conflicted with each other. First she was going to sell it, then she didn't want to lose clients. My neck grew so hot it could have turned water to steam.

Liam snorted. "You were unrecognizable. Don't blame us. You were the one acting like a lovesick idiot, chasing Jeremy Houston, your mortal enemy. Everyone in town saw it. We have a thousand eye witnesses who will attest to your insanity. Any jury will believe our side of the story. I had to protect my money. Fifty thousand dollars I put into that shop. I just wanted the money back. By not caring anymore, you were burning our investment like it was … something you cooked."

Ouch. Mean, very mean. And wrong! And crooked. Besides, I'd already given him a lot of his investment back, and more was likely on its way. That wasn't the point. "You swindled me while I was struggling. Forgery, theft, fraud."

Tennille stepped toward me and grabbed me by both hands. Her intent gaze pierced me, imploring. "It was fifty thousand dollars, Danica."

"I've whittled that number down to ten thousand or less over time. I guess we know the dollar amount on the price tag of your integrity." I dropped her hands and backed way. She reached for them and I swatted at her. "Forget it. I'll pay you back. Every cent." *When* and *how* would take some time. "Please, don't set foot in Candy Cane Cottage again."

"Danica!" Tennille's voice cracked. "I did it for Liam. He means everything to me."

"Nope." I turned my back on her and walked away. "Money means everything to you. Not just the business partnership, this friendship is over. You'll be hearing from my lawyer."

And possibly the police, though I hadn't decided about that. Mark would help me decide whether or not to press charges. Whoever he was, I already trusted him more than my so-called best friend. No wonder I hadn't liked her when we were teenagers. I should have trusted my instincts.

"Danica. I'm so sorry."

"Good. You should be."

Tears streamed down her face, but Liam was already taking their suitcases out of the car. He murmured complaints along the lines of *I'm going to kill Ivan. I bet I never see a penny of that investment. I'll sue her for it if she doesn't return it. It'll be her word against ours.*

There was no arguing with Liam ever, but especially not when he was worked up like this. Or reverting in my heart to a place where I could trust Tennille. I got back on my bicycle and coasted down the steep hill, but I couldn't muster any joy for the thrill.

When I came to a bend in the road, momentum wrenched control of me, and I didn't make the curve. The wheels skidded on an icy patch and flew out from under me. I toppled, sliding sideways on the asphalt for about ten yards. My yoga pants shredded, and so did the skin beneath them.

Ouch. Road rash covered my whole right flank. Shock kept the pain from setting in immediately, and I was able to stand up—sort of—hobbling and picking up my bike for a second before dropping it again.

The pedal that had taken the underside of the wreck was bent at a wince-worthy angle. Oh, and the handlebars had twisted ninety degrees.

There was no way I could ride it home. And I was in no condition to walk. My leg started to sting like it was making friends with a wasp's nest. But I had to keep moving. If I plopped down on that inviting patch of grass, I might not get up again.

What to do? Calling the ambulance was over the top.

Calling Mom and Dad would only make them ask questions I didn't want to answer. Telling them about Tennille's betrayal and the near loss of Candy Cane Cottage would take careful verbiage, which I hadn't had time to concoct.

I looked up and down the Christmas-decorated street full of houses of strangers not of my neighborhood. Finally, I called the only person I could think of who had a truck and could load my bike into the bed. This time, he picked up.

"Jeremy? Can you help me?"

Chapter 7

My bike was toast, but Jeremy loaded it in the back of his truck anyway.

Then, he lifted me up and set me carefully in the passenger seat, even taking time to make sure I was belted in. While he reached across me to click the latch, I took in his cologne. Its fragrance infiltrated my brain, smashing me once again with déjà vu—including an irrational longing for the man I'd detested for over a decade.

Upon reflection, hating him might have been a waste of my time and energy.

At my house, he carried me to a secure and comfortable place. He laid me on my side on the sofa, and said, "Don't take this the wrong way, but the best course of action here is to cut away some of the fabric so we can clean the wound."

All I could do at this point was to nod. The impact of the road rash was blooming into something more severe than I would have expected, and tears stung the corners of my eyes. I closed them and waited while he somehow managed to expose the scraped skin without compromising my modesty.

"Before I clean it and disinfect it, we'd better do something about the pain." Moments later, he emerged from my bathroom, carrying tweezers and an aerosol can of something that ended with –*caine,* and he gave my bare leg and hip a swift spray with the cold mist.

Within seconds, the pain began to subside, and I exhaled.

"You all right for some discomfort?"

"I just endured the most physical discomfort I've been through in ages." Probably. I couldn't remember the Episode Between and whether or not I'd needed painkillers after the fall on my head. "With that spray, I'm ready for anything."

"You're braver than I thought." He pulled a half smile, and next thing I knew, he and his tweezers had plucked about ten dozen bits of gravel out of my skin, all while he hummed a Christmas song, as if it could distract me a bit.

It did.

Meanwhile, numbed and humiliated, I stared at the lights on my Christmas tree, glancing at Jeremy now and then, hard at work as he cured me. How had this happened? How had Jeremy Houston had become my emergency contact—of all people in my life?

An hour later, he had covered me with a sheet, brought me several bags of frozen peas which he'd strategically placed along my wounded parts, and a big glass of water. He sipped from a Styrofoam gas station cup.

"Pepsi?" I ventured. For whatever reason, I associated him with that cola. "Never Coke?"

"Always Pepsi," he said, giving me a meaningful look that he held a little longer than I would've expected.

"With that stare, you're not trying to nudge me to remember something that happened right after my accident are you? Something about Pepsi? Because that whole two-month period of my life is a locked door."

"The Pepsi thing isn't recent." Again with the soulful look.

"Okay." I held out the *ay*. "It's a good drink, if a little stiff on the caffeine for this late in the day. Not that I'm judging."

"It was your idea."

Mine! "Seriously, I have zero recollection of our time together. The photos I took are from a parallel universe Now Me never entered."

"Like I said, the Pepsi isn't from that time period," he repeated.

When I didn't respond or act like this rang a bell, he pivoted. "You should tell me what happened on your bike, and why you called me instead of your parents when you crashed. Are they out of town?"

So I'd inconvenienced him. Ugh. "It's like this." Everything about my visit with Tennille spewed forth. "Which is why I couldn't tell my parents," I finished up. "They're going to be really hurt by what she did. Her mother and mine were like Siamese twins growing up."

"From what I remember, you and Tennille were never close when we were in school."

"No, that happened later. About the time I came back to Wilder River after college. She'd just gotten married to Liam, and she needed a job. She'd been a cheerleader and knew some gymnastics skills. It seemed like a good fit to hire her as a teacher when I first started coaching and rented time at the rec center."

"And when did she end up becoming a partner?"

"When I bought the property." It had only been a few weeks after I returned to Wilder River, and I often lumped them into the same moment, though there'd been a lapse.

"I need more details. So, she and her husband own some of the business? The building itself?"

"No, I bought the Candy Cane Cottage outright, at the auction. She and her husband supplied the seed money for the startup. Computers, utilities, advertising, coaches, certification, all of that. They've earned more than half their investment back, since we created the online content and sold the modules and started private coaching times. And I've repaid them on a set timetable, and they know it. It's not like they're out all that money." In fact, we'd earned back our investment twice as fast as the terms of the startup had indicated. Liam stood to double his money, so why he was freaking out, I had no idea. I told Jeremy all of this.

Jeremy took a long drink from his straw. "What do you want me to do?"

"Have you heard from Mark?" I sipped the ice water he'd brought me. So cooling.

"It's only been a few hours."

"Oh, right." Felt longer. "Can you advise me what I should do about the forged signature and whether I should, I don't know, press charges against them?"

"What does your gut say?"

"My gut says it's tawdry to send an ex-friend through the criminal justice system. Someone I'd loved. Someone I don't want to have bad feelings toward."

"Are you saying you'd like to forgive and forget?"

"More than anything!"

A soft, ironic chuckle issued from Jeremy. He set down his Pepsi and sat back in the chair. "Interesting."

"What's interesting?" I squinted at him. It was probably not very effective, due to my prone state. "Is it so impossible to think of me as someone who can forgive?"

With a slight shrug and tilt of his head, I had my answer.

Humph. I could forgive. I'd forgiven a lot of things. I frowned and wished I could turn away from him, but the bags of frozen peas held me captive.

Jeremy stood up, brushing off his jeans. "I'm going to go now."

What? He was leaving?

"Don't look so distraught. I thought you didn't like me. Doesn't it relieve you to not have to endure my company?"

Wow. That was probably how I'd made it seem the last few times we'd met, though. Not an inaccurate assessment of my former opinions. "I'm sorry about how I treated you right before Thanksgiving."

"You threw me out on my ear."

"Is it damaged? Can you lean over here so I can see it? Did you need stitches or anything? I hear ears bleed a lot. Almost as much as head wounds."

"Very funny." He offered me a smirk. "Look, I am glad to help you with this conundrum, but only if you want me to. I'm going to ask you one thing, though."

Oh, no. I'd been suckered into traps in the past. "What is it?" My wariness disrupted the good energy in the room.

"Fine." Jeremy held up his palms. "If you don't need help, that's all right. But know that the thing I'm asking isn't something horrifically hard."

"Just tell me what it is. I'll do it." That he really wouldn't hurt me, I knew in my heart. "Name it."

"Sometime before we meet again, look back through our text threads on your phone."

"Huh?" I reached for it off the coffee table and clutched it to my chest. "We communicated?" During the Between Episode? *What did I say to him?* Wince-cringe-gag. I'd had his number in my phone, obviously, and I'd texted him the other day—and received the *out of the office* reply.

"I take it from your attitude, you haven't read them already."

Accurate. "Okay," I managed, but it was hard to squeeze the word through my narrowing windpipe. "Thank you."

Jeremy walked to the front door, where he paused. "I'd be willing to bring you dinner tonight. Just message me and let me know what you'd like." And before I could answer with *Chinese food*, or *homemade soup*, he'd slipped through the front door and shut it.

His truck's engine fired up, and the gravel crunched as he drove away, leaving me on my sofa in the glow of my undecorated Christmas tree.

Dinner. He'd bring me dinner? I just had to tell him what I'd like?

If I messaged him and put in a dinner order before I got hungry, that meant I'd have the threads open. And he demanded I read them first, before we met again. Which mean, I'd have to devour those texts right away. Like, as in now.

Was I ready to examine what my non-self-self had said to Jeremy Houston?

Nope. Not remotely.

Chapter 8

An hour later, my stomach growled. My hip and side were getting frostbite. Well, not exactly. The peas had thawed and turned mushy, but my skin was cold. I set down my historical novel and repositioned, turning to lie on my back. I pushed all the little bags of peas up against my side, but several fell off onto the floor—*plunk, thunk.*

Ouch. I needed some painkillers, more of that spray. I reached for the aerosol can Jeremy had left on the table. Slowly, I peeled back the sheet covering my side. Ouch. Some of its fabric had stuck to the wounded areas. Ouch, ouch, ouch. The higher the thread count, the more threads that could stick to an owie.

When I tried to spray the stuff, I missed, turned the nozzle around and aimed it toward my face. A few droplets got in my eye.

Geez! Ouch! It smelled like antiseptic, and heepie jeepie that hurt! Using a corner of the sheet, I swiped some out, and clearly—*clearly*—I was not up to the task of caring for myself during this convalescence tonight.

Tomorrow, perhaps. But for now, I was a living, breathing bruise.

What choice did I have? I texted Jeremy.

I'm taking you up on your offer, if you have time. How about those roast beef mini-panini sandwiches with provolone and grilled mushrooms from The Hot Chocolate Shoppe, say, in an hour?

The next text took courage to send: *I'll start reading the texts now.*

And then, I scrolled upward, to the top of a very long history of texts. It would be better to look through them chronologically, to maybe get an idea of how things had evolved.

Whoa. It was almost an infinite scroll. How many times could two people text each other in a few weeks? Hundreds, apparently. Possibly over a thousand. The sheer volume!

Even more unbelievable, most of them were from me, not the other way around.

What was the term the older gymnastics students used for girls who overdid their attention for a guy to the point of ridiculousness? Simp? Whatever. I'd been that slang girl if ever anyone had.

I must have hit my head harder than I thought.

Jeremy! I'm dying for another chapter in the book. If I don't find out what happens next, I'll just expire.

Seriously? And what book was it? The only book I'd ever felt like I'd die if I didn't hear what happened next was *Jane Eyre*. My Between Episode self wouldn't have known that.

Jeremy, can you come again for a chapter? It's so boring here, and they keep turning on my television. I'm about to wring their necks from my sick bed.

Hi. What are you doing right now?

Finally, one from Jeremy: *Chopping wood at Aunt June's house. Woodpile for the winter.*

Oh, merciful heavens. I did not need an image of Jeremy Houston as a lumberjack chain-sawing a trail through the forest of my brain right now. I was having a hard enough time keeping my physical reactions to him wholesome.

Can you come see me when you finish up?

I'll have to shower first. It's Indian summer temperatures out here today.

Nope. The only thing I needed less than mental pictures of a sweaty, exercising Jeremy Houston, was images of a showering Jeremy Houston.

I skipped a few texts—just to keep everything G-rated.

There were some things about whatever book it was again, and then a huge clue—a reference to Sinjin and Mr. Rochester. What? No. Jeremy had read me *Jane Eyre?*

Um, okay. I shifted on the sofa, my skin and ears buzzing.

Then another level of this miracle whacked me with a two-by-four.

The guy had discovered my favorite book and read it aloud to me while I was sick and bored in the hospital and probably had something like double vision from the head injury and couldn't read to myself? While I didn't even know Grandma Candalaria's name? My favorite novel was not one of those well-known facts, not something I told every passing stranger.

Could Jeremy read my very soul? My inner, deepest soul? The one even I hadn't known?

Tears pricked at the corners of my eyes for the second time today, but this time not from pain but from something far deeper inside me. Something I wasn't ready to acknowledge.

I devoured the rest of the texts, spiraling into them, drinking up the blossoming romance between us as it clearly grew day by day. There were a lot of late-night texting threads. In one, we'd apparently spent half the night texting each other silly ideas for restaurants someone could open in Wilder River during tourist season, including how to staff them. Another night, I'd kept him on his phone into the wee hours discussing art I'd studied in a coffee table book he'd brought me, with Jeremy telling me all about the artists, their history and painting styles.

Exactly who *was* this guy?

By the time I reached the last few days of our correspondence before my memory came back, I felt like I'd been reading a love story for a slow-burn romance, like the one between Elizabeth Bennet and Mr. Darcy. Every time I'd asked for help, Jeremy had been there for me. He'd even taken me fishing—in the moonlight. I'd texted him a gusher-load of thanks for that the next day, telling him not a few times how much I was longing to see him again soon, and to kiss him again as soon as possible.

I guessed that the texts slowed down based on the fact we were spending a lot more hours in the day together at that point. Texts came before eight in the morning every day, and then they resumed around two the next morning. Wow. We'd been together a lot. And our conversations were increasingly emotionally intimate. I'd shared with him all my fears about regaining—or not regaining—my memories. How that would affect my relationships and my life.

All of Jeremy's responses had been hopeful, positive, reassuring. *Loving.*

A strange swelling expanded in my chest, a sensation I'd never felt before. This time, no déjà vu was attached, unfortunately. In fact, my brain and logic railed against it with a big *no! Not love for Jeremy Houston!*

But there it was—stark, bold, and undeniable in blue and white text bubbles on my phone screen. Some version of me had fallen hard for the current version of Jeremy.

I swiped at my cheeks, which were wet. I dabbed at them with the sheet.

"Hello?" Jeremy appeared at the door, his arms laden with bags and drink-holders, and came toward me. "Are you all right? Are you in pain? I'll bring you a painkiller right away."

This. *This* was the Jeremy from the texts. Warm, open and solicitous. *Mine.*

"I'm all right." What excuse could I give? "I accidentally sprayed that analgesic in my eye. I'm such a clod." It was true, just not recent or causative.

He gave me a questioning look but seemed to buy my fib. "Would you like to eat now?"

For the next few minutes, Jeremy attended to my immediate needs: painkillers and sustenance.

"This is really good." I took a second panini from the stack. "Getting in bike wrecks makes me ravenous." Combine it with an emotional roller coaster, and I was likely to eat all seven of the mini-paninis filled with roast beef and provolone. I looked at Jeremy before I bit into it, though. "Thank you."

Jeremy handed me a collared cup from the holder. "I hope you still like vanilla shots in your hot cocoa."

"Is that something you learned about me while I was ..."

"We never went to the Hot Chocolate Shoppe together."

"Then how did you know?"

He recounted an incident from years before. It involved hot cocoa with way too many peppermint shots, which had resulted in my dumping the cocoa on one of my mom's prize rosebush and killing it.

She hadn't been happy with Jeremy. Or with me, for that matter. But I was the one who'd dumped it, so I'd told her to quit being mad at Jeremy. She hadn't.

"I thought with all that peppermint you were playing a prank on me."

"But you hate pranks. You always have."

"Then why play them on me and my family all the time?" And ruin my sister's wedding, for instance?

Jeremy lowered his chin and gave me a penetrating stare. I'd never endured anything quite so intense. At last, he blinked and looked aside. "I brought you the paperwork."

"What paperwork?" I let the old subject drop, for now. But he owed me an explanation.

"Mark reviewed the contract with the forged signature—I let him know about that—and he sent a different one that rescinds all previous contracts, making them null and void. You'll sign it, and then Tennille and her husband will need to."

"Does it involve their admission of guilt?"

"If you would like me to have him add that, I can, but I wasn't sure what you'd want."

I didn't know that either. Even after getting plenty to eat. "I honestly can't remember anything from that period of time after my accident, so I don't know whether to insist they take responsibility or not. If I was acting truly crazy, I can kind of see where they were coming from, even though what they did was beyond wrong."

Obviously mulling it over, Jeremy sipped his cup of cocoa. It was the first time I'd ever seen him drink anything but Pepsi. "You can't remember anything?"

"Nothing at all. Nothing I said or did."

Jeremy lowered his chin and his voice. "Or felt."

There. That was the rub. Slowly, I shook my head, an apology scrunching my brow.

"I'd better get going." He set his cup on the table and stood. "You can handle the cleanup of dinner, right?" He brushed off his jeans and picked up his jacket. "You can walk around a little?"

"You're going?"

I think I expected him to offer to come back tomorrow, to read me more of *Jane Eyre*, to teach me to cook. Or at least to say his Aunt June needed him. Chores at her place had figured prominently in our texts.

Instead, he said, "Take care of yourself, Danica." And then he was gone.

It sounded so final.

I spent the rest of the evening rereading all our texts. And wishing.

Chapter 9

By the next morning, I could hobble around just fine. My mountain bike was out of order, possibly beyond repair—at least by me—but with enough Tylenol, I managed the three-mile walk to the Candy Cane Cottage. Tennille and Liam met me there, accompanied by a man in a rumpled three-piece suit who now sported a beard and therefore didn't look as much like Liam as did his biography picture online. However, the resemblance was still obvious.

"Ivan Rutledge." He stuck out his hand, but I didn't take it. This was not a friendly meeting. "You're the famous Danica Denton."

"Usually she's really nice." Tennille winced, cowering behind Liam. "Let's just get started."

Instead of looking at the contract themselves, they handed it straight to Ivan. Then, Tennille shifted her weight back and forth for the duration of Ivan's perusal, while Liam scrolled his phone. It was so *Liam* of him.

"This contract has no teeth." Ivan looked up. Then he bumped his shoulder against Liam's causing him to drop his phone.

The screen cracked in a spider web pattern. Liam cursed. "Ivan, you son of a gun."

Ivan snatched the phone from Liam's grip and shoved it in his own pocket. "Why'd you make me drive all the way down here at this inhuman hour of the morning when all this contract does is negate the earlier one?" Ivan's teeth were clenched. "I'm charging you double my hourly rate."

"We're *family!* Doesn't that mean anything to you? We could have been facing criminal charges, thanks to you. You're the one who said to sign her name, since she was so out of it."

So that was it. I exhaled. Tennille hadn't been the mastermind behind defrauding me, this crooked lawyer had.

"You're the one who wanted his money back and told me to do whatever it took."

Liam muttered some choice phrases.

I had no patience for this crooked lawyer. "Tell them to sign it immediately." I planted my fists on my hips. "And if I hear that you sent them a bill for your so-called services, I'll report you to the state bar for encouraging illegal activity."

"You have no evidence," Ivan challenged, but he handed Liam and Tennille each a pen, and then stepped aside so they could place the new contract on the countertop and sign it. "And how could you afford the help of Landmark Legal? Mark charges exorbitant prices." He turned to Liam. "I told you she was embezzling from the business and you could have gotten your investment back much swifter. You're getting duped, cousin. Take her to court. I'll be glad to represent you."

Tennille wound up and punched Ivan in the jaw. He reeled backward and fell on his tailbone on the polished concrete floor. "Stay away from my husband." She crouched into fighting stance.

Wow. Apparently, all those hours training in jiu-jitsu really paid off when it mattered.

"I'll sue you for assault." He rubbed his chin, his face bright red.

"Go ahead and try." Liam grabbed him by the collar and jerked him to his feet. "Say one more thing to my wife—ever—and I'll call Grandma."

For the first time, true fear entered Ivan's face.

I had no idea who Liam and Ivan's grandma was, but Ivan backed up, his palms forward in surrender. "Fine. Just forget it." Ivan left, trailing a cloud of filth, kind of like that comic book character kid who never bathed.

Tennille threw her arms around me and fell on my neck, weeping. "Danica." Several sobs. "I couldn't sleep all night. I never meant for any of this to happen." More crying. "I was so worried about you, but Liam was upset, and then we saw Ivan at the family Veterans Day picnic. He and Liam shared a few too many drinks, and a couple of days later, they were shoving paperwork at me, saying, 'This is the only way to get our investment back, since it seems like Danica is never going to be herself again.' I was scared. About everything."

"Fear makes us do the wrong thing a lot of the time." At last, I returned her hug. "It's all over now."

"You're not going to call the cops on us?"

No, but I also didn't trust her again yet. "I'll pay you back the remainder of your investment immediately, and we can end our partnership. That seems like the best move for now."

"But you don't have it. It's almost ten thousand dollars."

"I'll get it." I'd take out an equity loan on the building. It'd increased in value a lot over the past few years. "I'll return the money with interest."

For the first time, Liam looked up. "No, you won't." He shoved his broken phone in his pocket. He must have gotten it back from Ivan before Ivan took off. "Look, we owe you more than an apology. I was a knucklehead. Being around Ivan makes me more of one. Drinking makes it worse." He shook his head. "We'll forfeit the remainder of the investment. It's the least we can do for all you've forgiven us."

That wasn't right, either. Eventually I'd work out something that was fair to both of us that I felt good about. For now, we agreed to dissolve our Candy Cane Cottage business partnership.

Liam went to their car, but Tennille lingered.

"When we were packing up to leave, Liam was saying it might be good for us to get out of Wilder River. We've never really lived anywhere else. Sometimes staying in a place too long makes it so we don't really grow. The disaster we caused you might be just the open door we need to make some changes."

"You're an amazing seamstress, Tennille. You could have a sewing business."

"If I lived in a bigger city, I could teach jiu-jitsu full time."

"You'd be amazing."

"I'd rather work with adults." She wrinkled her nose. "Kids all day? Not really my thing."

"That's so hard for me to relate to. I'd rather spend all day with kids."

Tennille gurgled. "You should have some of your own, and then see how you feel about it." She rolled her eyes. "Other people's kids are a lot less appealing once you've been mom-mom-mom-mom-mom nonstop for years." She frowned. "Sorry. I know you want to be a mom more than anything. That was insensitive of me."

"Yeah, it's okay."

"How about Jeremy? Is he an option?"

"For what?" I knew what she was getting at. But she had no idea how hurt he'd looked the few times I'd interacted with him lately. And yet how stoic he'd been. Confident but hurt—was that a thing? I quit faking ignorance of her meaning. "I don't think Jeremy Houston is an option."

"Oh, come on." She rolled her eyes. "He sent you flowers. Looks like he paid your legal fees. And that's just the stuff you can remember."

If Tennille had had any inkling of those texts, she would have been shrieking over the possibilities of me and Jeremy. "He's not the guy he used to be."

"He was never the guy you thought he was, you know. He didn't pull a prank at Angelica's wedding, at least not on purpose. In fact, it wasn't a prank at all. Plus, from what I heard around town, he thinks Angelica was born with a bum leg. He's got no idea her injury was caused by someone thinking they were funny."

"Who told you that?" The memory of the wedding always turned me bristly. How would Tennille know what Jeremy's intentions that night had been? "Whose side are you on?"

"Yours."

Liam honked. Tennille hugged me and left.

I looked around Candy Cane Cottage. The assistant coaches were all in teaching mode. The energy was good—constant, actually. I had grown to love it here, despite its starting out as a way to live out Mom and Dad's dreams for Angelica. But Tennille might be right. Staying in one place might keep a person from growth.

Jeremy had left—and he'd obviously grown. He wasn't the insufferable mess-up I'd known as a kid. In fact, he might not have ever been a prankster, from the look on his face last night when he'd said *You don't like pranks.*

He knew a lot about me. It turned out, there were a lot of things I needed to know about Jeremy and his past—and not just about during the period of time I couldn't remember.

Besides, I owed him an apology, and a huge debt of thanks.

I sent him a text.

Are you in town? Would you like to have dinner with me?

Chapter 10

It took the remainder of the day. It also involved several failed attempts, a kitchen trash can full of mistakes, and a lot of wasted food, but I finally ended up with pan-fried chicken, greens, and a batch of biscuits that didn't require me to shut off the smoke detector. I set out the food on the dining room table.

Just in time, too. Jeremy rang my doorbell.

When I opened the door, my breath caught. The contours of his handsome face were even better looking because of the goodness that shone from his soul. A breeze whooshed through, as Jeremy walked past me into the house, bringing the scent of his cologne with it.

Whap! I had to lean against the door of the hall closet. My body chemistry reacted to Jeremy's pheromones like they were a powerful drug against which I had no defenses. I trailed after him. My head spun, filling with scent memories, and then with what might be actual memories.

A kiss, a tumble, my head hitting the floor.

We entered the living room, and I fixated on the spot between the couch and the coffee table. The back of my head throbbed. The memory of Jeremy's face came into focus. My lips burned.

Was I remembering something?

"Did you cook?" Jeremy stopped and turned around, and I plowed into him. "Whoa, there." He steadied me. Then, setting down some bags he'd brought and holding me by the shoulders he examined me carefully. "Are you okay?"

No. Not remotely. "I—I think I remembered something."

"Usually people say that another way: *I think I forgot something.*" His eyes crinkled at the sides. "It looks like you forgot you can't cook. It smells really good in here." He turned and looked at the place settings on the table. "This looks really good."

"You told me if I kept trying I could learn something new."

Slowly he nodded. "I did say that. But …"

But he hadn't said it since my memories had returned. "I'm sorry." I shook myself. "I'm having … a moment. And it's making me forget my manners. Please, have a seat. Dinner's ready. I owe you thanks and apologies, and this—for what it's worth—is my attempt at all that."

Instead of seating himself, he helped me into a chair at the table. Jeremy, the gentleman. I marveled again.

"I'm impressed," he said, surveying the meal again. "You baked and cooked."

"It was a process of elimination. You'll notice there's no pasta salad."

"Um, okay. I hadn't been expecting one."

"You should, since that was in the picture. You made pasta salad, chicken, biscuits, and greens for me." I pulled out my phone and showed him. "I wanted to recreate it."

He peered at the screen of my phone, frowning. "Is there some reason you chose that particular meal?"

"Besides the fact it looked like the easiest one? Yes. But let's say grace so we can eat before it gets cold."

Jeremy and I bowed our heads and he offered the prayer. Then he took the first bite while I held my breath and watched, pushing away even the swirl of memories vying for my attention. This moment was too critical. For some reason, it felt like everything hung on it.

"It's good," he said through the bite of chicken. "You seasoned it really well."

I took a bite. Whoa. Very salty. I took a sip of water. "You're exaggerating. It's at the edge of inedible."

"And yet, it *is* edible. Good work." He took another bite, and a big gulp of water.

"I should have bought some Pepsi for you." I'd obviously never be quite as aware of his needs as he was of mine. "Answer me this—why the Pepsi obsession?" I took a bite of the biscuit. A little dry but, again, edible.

"You honestly don't remember?" He set down his fork and knife. "That day in sixth grade? Everyone was on my case for the paper clip incident."

"I remember the incident. What does it have to do with Pepsi?"

"Seriously?" He stared at me, mouth open. Finally, he said, "I was about to be lynched by a mob of twelve-year-olds because we'd all been sentenced to three consecutive recess periods with our heads on our desks. Mrs. Underwood, Liam's mom, left the room. You went over to her desk, took her Pepsi, and brought it to me."

I'd stolen my teacher's caffeine? "I did not do that."

"You absolutely did. *Here, drink this. It'll calm you down,* you said."

Wisps of that moment floated at the edges of my mind. "I used to babysit for a lady with a crazy-active six-year-old. She'd give him Pepsi and he'd settle right down. I must have thought it would work for you."

"You admitted to taking it when she came back in and asked. You got detention in the principal's office."

My memory of it was too cloudy. "Did the Pepsi help you?"

"Yeah. It helped that day. For a few years, my parents told me no, I couldn't drink it, that it wasn't a kid drink. I think they assumed the combo of sugar and caffeine would only make my ADHD worse, but I bought it from the school vending machine in high school. When I joined the military, I started drinking it every morning. My focus improved greatly, as did my results."

Ah, so he'd been successful in the military. An image of Jeremy

Houston in uniform tempted me. I suppressed a little sigh.

"I've been drinking it ever since anytime I need to stay focused and calm. When I forget it, my brain goes into a whirlwind of thoughts, and I can't pick one to focus on. Having an overactive mind is helpful when I want to brainstorm lots of unique ideas, but not so helpful when I need to buckle down and work."

Wow. I'd helped him. And he'd become successful. Based on Pepsi.

Weird. But kind of sweet.

"Thanks for taking the punishment and getting detention for me, Danica." My name on his lips did something to me that should be illegal.

"It's fine." I gulped. "I don't even remember detention. Oh, wait." Yes, I did remember. "Yeah. They stuck me in detention in the school library. That's when I found out how much I love the book *Jane Eyre*. I read almost the whole thing over those three days. I was mad when detention ended, because I still hadn't figured out the mystery in the book. I didn't get a chance to check it out, and I was stuck the whole weekend wondering about the fire."

Wow. Pepsi and *Jane Eyre* were connected.

Make that, Jane and Pepsi connected me to Jeremy.

Pulsations covered me from head to toe.

I stared at him, and the intrusive memories of a moment ago became insistent. They broke through my concentration and took over, flooding me with a sensory overload of Jeremy's kiss, his arms around me, my intensifying feelings for him. I couldn't push them away.

They pelted me incessantly, and I could barely sit still. There was just one cure—and I'd need Jeremy's help, and only Jeremy's help. Would Jeremy be game? Considering all the recent times I'd rejected him?

Argh. I chickened out. He went over near the door and picked up the bags he'd brought with him. From inside, he pulled a cellophane-front box with pretty Christmas ornaments. "Give me a hand?" he said.

I got up, and together we added better Christmas cheer to my tree. There were all kinds of cute figurines—which he'd chosen. For me. And my tree. And for the hominess of my home.

An ache for him blossomed in my chest. To quell it, I told him about Tennille and Liam and their decision to move. "They're leaving Wilder River, it seems."

"She actually admitted to not liking working with children?" His brows raised.

Interesting that he'd focus on that point. "Yep, in no uncertain terms."

"I can't imagine. Kids are so great. And they're drawn to you. I hope you're not thinking about following her lead."

I stifled a gasp. "Stop teaching the kids?"

Jeremy let out a laugh. "There's the Danica I know."

And love, my wishful thinking filled in the blanks. It was weird every time I realized how well he knew me.

"I mentioned that I had another reason for making that meal." We were done with the tree and had gone back to the table, where our dinner had cooled.

"Yeah?" Jeremy broke off a piece of biscuit and tasted it. And took another drink of water. Couldn't blame him.

The moment had arrived. I bolstered my nerve, and the request tumbled from my lips. "Dr. Chen said if I revisited some of the circumstances that I'd been experiencing during the period of time I'd lost, I might regain some of my memories of it."

"So you made the same dinner you cooked that night?"

Wait. What? "*I* cooked that night?"

"Yeah, it was your first meal to make solo. Well, I pan-fried the chicken, but seasoned it and you made everything else."

No way. "You're kidding." I took another bite. It tasted a whole lot better all of a sudden—and it jarred loose another faint remembrance. "Did I also bake a cake?"

"Yes, and you layered it with ice cream."

"Jeremy!" I put down my utensils and placed my palms flat on the tablecloth. "I can cook!" Then the full understanding washed through me, and I spoke more softly. "You taught me to cook."

For a second, he eyed me. He wiped his mouth with a napkin. "You put in the work."

I had? If only I could remember! If only I could capture more of the pieces of what happened. They floated nearby, but I had no net to collect them.

Try reenacting some of the activities you know you participated in—with the people who were there, Dr. Chen had said, implying my brain may cooperate.

The cooking had done so. What about other things? It was too cold for tennis or golf now. My bike was ruined, if we'd biked together. I'd ridden in his truck without recalling anything specific.

That left … kissing.

"Jeremy, I need your help."

"I get that a lot from you." He said it good-naturedly, bless him. "What now, Danica?" He pronounced my name like it was a substitute for *milady*.

"I need you to kiss me."

"Is that so?" Jeremy's face didn't betray any emotion, blast it.

"And not just a peck on the cheek. I need us to kiss like we were kissing when my amnesia disappeared."

144

Chapter 11

Why Jeremy was lying back on the sofa and looking at me expectantly, I had no clue. This was not how it happened.

"I don't get it. When I woke up, you were smashing me against the floor." At least that's how the lay of the land had been when I'd come to my senses.

"Don't let this offend your prudish sensibilities, but you leaped on top of me, and we tumbled." He pointed at the ground beside the couch.

I closed my eyes, squeezing them against his words. "Are you just saying that to deceive me with another one of your pranks?"

He sat up. "You keep saying I am a prankster. I'm not."

Oh, right. "What do you call my near heart-attack when you left that big cut-out cardboard figure of Ken Railings in my shower?"

"That was meant to make you happy. He was your favorite member of The Aussie Boys."

"But what about this?" I pointed to the chipped molar again. "You planted a rock in a snack just to trick me into needing dental work. Not cool."

"I have no idea how that gravel got in there, I swear. You had seemed sad that day, and I bought the brownie at the gas station. It was before I learned to cook."

He knew brownies were a comfort food? Well, that was a given.

Besides, I was on a roll, though, not listening to weak excuses. "Or how you ruined my sister's wedding? That was the last straw, you know."

Jeremy sat forward on the couch, placed his elbows on his spread knees, and put his head in his hands. "So you haven't forgiven me."

"Tennille says I should."

"You're trusting Tennille now? Taking her advice?" He turned his head to give me an annoyed look. "All right, forget I said that. You shouldn't ignore good advice just because it issues from a bad place."

"Tennille isn't so bad."

"You can forgive her for defrauding you of your life's work, but you can't forgive me for throwing pebbles at a window so I could serenade you?"

"You broke the window." While singing my favorite pop ballad, but my parents had been irritated, and I'd had to give up my babysitting money to pay for the repair.

"Or for giving you vegetables in a doughnuts box?"

"Wasn't that a subtle *you need to eat healthier* message?"

"Danica, you preferred vegetables to doughnuts, and everyone else was giving people doughnuts that Valentine's Day, per the Wilder River High tradition. I didn't want you to feel left out."

Everyone had snickered behind their hands about his prankish way to say I was fat. I knew he hadn't meant that, but the words of others had soured me on the gesture. They shouldn't have. After that, I'd started eating Little Debbie Cakes just to "fix" my taste buds to fit in.

Jeremy went on, "Or for taking Penelope's advice and trying to impress you with a *Grease 2* movie moment, which unintentionally took you away from the wedding on my motorcycle?"

To get him out of there, I'd ridden on the back of the bike. My hands on his hips had felt right, and I'd been so confused I'd yelled at him more ferociously than I ever intended to.

I blinked. I breathed in and out. "Penelope told you to ruin Angelica's wedding?"

"No!" Jeremy threw his hands up. "No one told me to ruin a

146

wedding. The throttle slipped as I hit a rut in the grass of your back yard, and the bike lost control, knocked over the tent pole and the swan ice sculpture and landed us all in the pool. It was an accident."

"You were trying to do something nice for me?" Because *Grease 2* had been my favorite throwback movie as a teenager?

"I was trying to show you someone *saw* you, knew what you loved and what you hated, cared about you, instead of always making you be in the shadow of your older sister's needs. I wanted you to be the star of the moment for once. I was sick and tired of how your family always put Angelica first." He exhaled sharply.

My head spun. Truly, my parents did *always* put Angelica first, then and now. But she'd been injured. She legitimately needed to be first. "She needed them more." My retort sounded small, weak.

"Just because one child is born with a disability doesn't mean the other kids in the family don't deserve attention. Every time I went to your house, your family was doing something that revolved around Angelica. It was never, ever about you. And I knew it should be."

"You"—I frowned—"weren't playing a prank."

"I wasn't. You hate pranks."

"I do."

"Why do you?"

"Honestly? You have no idea?" I'd better clear up any false notion. "Angelica wasn't born with a disability. She was injured when someone played a prank on her."

"What are you talking about?" Jeremy exhaled, clearly disbelieving my statement. "She could never walk. Not for as long as I knew her."

"You moved here when you and I were in eleven, Jeremy. It happened a long time before that."

He just blinked, so I went on, "She was ten, and I was five. She was taking gymnastics at the old gym, Tumbleweeds, and someone thought it would be really funny to slather the balance beam with vegetable shortening, make it slick, to see someone biff it. Well,

147

Angelica did. She fell hard, causing more than a simple break. It turned out her bones were brittle. The fall broke her femur, her hip, and her pelvis in five places. She spent six months in a wheelchair, and another year learning to walk again."

"I never knew."

"You couldn't have known." I explained how Mom and Dad had asked the community not to talk about the injury but only to cheer her on. There had been rallies, fundraisers, a parade in her honor. Everyone had been her cheerleaders, the whole town.

Jeremy sighed. "No wonder you hate pranks."

"I am sorry I wildly misinterpreted your intentions on her wedding day." I couldn't have known that he didn't know about Angelica's accident. "It just seemed …"

"Seemed like everyone should be celebrating Angelica."

"Well, to be fair, it was her wedding."

He heaved a sigh. "That's a reasonable point." Now, he broke into a smile. "You're right that I was a screw-up. But most of the time, my gaffes were only around you."

"I didn't really know you, Jeremy." Not the guy he'd been as a kid, nor the guy he'd become as an adult—thanks to the healing powers of Pepsi, apparently. Floods of attraction washed through me for him. There was a lot more to Jeremy Houston than I'd ever begun to give him credit for. "I'm sorry about that most of all."

"I think if you did, you'd like me." He touched my hand. "I'm a decent guy."

"That much I'm certain of." I trembled at his touch. I didn't know him, but I was aching to change that. I was falling for him, and he must have seen it in my eyes.

In an instant, Jeremy's curled fingers were beneath my chin, lifting it, and his lips were on mine. A soft kiss, a tender half-second. Not nearly long enough to jar any memories loose. "Send me a message next time you want to see me."

Could I send it five seconds after he left? All the messages we'd shared before sparkled like diamonds intricately cut and catching the light.

He touched my shoulder and slid his hand down my arm, stopping at my fingers, which he pressed. "Thank you for dinner."

And he was gone.

Chapter 12

"**D**anica? Are you home?" Angelica's voice cut the morning air. "I heard you were in a bicycle accident, and I came to help you."

I wedged myself up off the couch, onto one elbow. "What? What are you doing here? You're supposed to have surgery tomorrow. Don't you have pre-ops? I'm driving to Reedsville to help you."

"They postponed it. I asked them to. And you can't drive yet—plus, this second accident! Look at you."

This did not compute. I rubbed my eyes and fixed my ponytail, which had fallen into disrepair. "I'm sorry, what? What's going on?" My eye fell on the clock. Ten already?

Friday. The gymnastics showcase was tomorrow—and all the parents would be there, but Tennille wouldn't. Geez. I had to get moving and do all the final preparation, get the mats hauled to the rec center, make sure the lighting was set.

Ouch. The bruising was for real today.

Angelica looked around the room. "Someone ate dinner and left it on the table."

Oh, right. Last night loomed. "I meant to clean up. My hip just hurts, and I figured since I live alone it would keep until morning."

Angelica got up and went straight to work, clearing the table, filling the sink with hot water, and putting away everything I'd left in a mess. "This looks like date food. Did a man cook dinner for you without cleaning up, and then stay too *late?*"

"Actually, if anything, he left too early." After that, I'd stayed in a dismayed lump on the couch for the rest of the night, dreaming of him.

"Too early for what?" Angelica loaded the silverware into the dishwasher rack. "Is it serious? Who is this guy? Mom and Dad hinted you've been acting strange lately."

Great. "The surgery, Angelica. What's going on with your surgery?"

"Oh, that. It's not safe to undergo when you're pregnant."

Now, I jumped off the sofa and made a beeline for my sister, my bruising pain evaporated. I threw my arms around her and jumped until I nearly knocked her off her feet. "A baby? You're going to be a mother?"

The words slugged me like a boxing glove in the gut, despite the fact I was happy beyond everything for Angelica and Brady.

"I'm so confused." For the past few years, they'd kept postponing parenthood until this planned hip and leg surgery. "What happened?"

"We just miscalculated, I guess. But we're so happy!"

Me, too—honestly—if it was possible to be happy for and insanely envious of someone simultaneously. I felt no closer to being a mom today than I'd been when Angelica got married ten years ago, and I'd surrounded myself with other people's children to fill the gaping hole in me. Now, Angelica had a husband and a growing family, and I was just left on the sidelines again.

"Mom asked me to come up to Wilder River so you can plan my baby shower."

"Me?" So the visit wasn't to help me heal after my accident. "Oh, great. I'd love to. When should we have it? Everyone in the family will be in town for Christmas." That was just two weeks off, so I'd have to work fast, and—

We dove into discussing dates, guest list, themes, gift registry, refreshments. Everything Angelica had always dreamed of.

"Don't look so exhausted by this." She patted my arm. "You've got other things going on in your life, probably."

Good point. The showcase was tomorrow, and … Jeremy. Angelica had no idea. I found the cabinet with the Tylenol and took a couple with a cup of water.

"I'm not exhausted." Lie. "I'm happy for you."

"Well, show some spirit. Your older sister's having a baby!" She gave me a smile. "It's what I've been waiting for my whole life."

"Yeah, me too."

"Right?" Angelica squeezed my hand. "You'll be the best aunt."

I'd meant my own children. She'd meant hers. Was Jeremy correct that my world had been forced to orbit Angelica's?

If it had, it'd been by my own consent. Well, I did love my sister. This was her moment.

"You do owe me this baby shower. And there'd better be no motorcycles at it."

"Guaranteed." Mostly because Jeremy didn't come around uninvited. *These days, I ask.* Would I ask?

"Look, Angelica, you should know something about that disaster at your wedding." I told her Jeremy's side of the legendary motorcycle incident, although not his full reasoning, not the stuff she wouldn't take kindly, like he meant them. "I think he was trying to impress me with a grand gesture. Penelope's idea." Or show me I was important, more like.

Rather than being gracious, or even laughing, she contorted her lips into a frown. "Suddenly you're sympathizing with the enemy?"

"You were best friends with his older sister Penelope."

"Maybe, but if I'd known she put her brother up to that, I never would have spoken to her again. Take her name off the baby shower guest list."

"She lives in India. She's not coming to your baby shower."

Angelica's lips formed a pout. "She might be home for the holidays and show up." We'd settled on the afternoon of Christmas Eve for the shower, since the most family members would be around. "Fine. I will have to have words with her about it, though—just to verify this jerk isn't lying to you."

"He's not lying." And he wasn't a jerk. Far from it. The farthest of any guy I'd ever met, in fact.

"You like him." Angelica leaned forward. We were at the well-cleaned dining room table with scraps of paper and notebooks filled with ideas between us. "What strange universe is this? I've heard you were gallivanting about the country club with some handsome guy, but please, *please* say it's not Jeremy Houston!"

Deflect, deflect, deflect! "Where would you hear a thing like that?"

"I saw Rufus Swalwell at a Rhinos game." Wow. That guy got around. And he had a penchant for gossip about me. Angelica and Brady had season tickets for the hockey team. "He just came up and warned me that my sister was getting some action."

My face and neck burned. "Is that what people are saying?"

"I told him to put a cork in it."

"Thanks." I could count on Angelica to defend me. A little. If Tennille had been there, she might have punched him in the jaw. "I'm not dating Jeremy Houston." Not now, anyway. "But he was here last night."

"Jeremy Houston is the cause of the mess in this house?"

"I made him dinner."

Angelica burst into laughter. "You? You cooked?"

"Not particularly well, honestly. Too much salt." I was getting tired of this conversation. "Look, a lot of things have happened to me lately. I might not be the same person I was a few months ago."

"I'll say." Angelica pushed her chair back from the table. "You're getting hurt all the time. Is this a ploy to get attention?"

And if it were? "Are you upset with me for wrecking on my mountain bike?"

"At least you had the opportunity to ride a bike."

Not this again. "I'm not cleared to drive. I have to walk

everywhere I go for now." And it was getting colder. "Look, I've got the gymnastics showcase to prepare for. It's tomorrow." And I needed to shower and dress my road-rash wound. I'd been wearing loose dresses since the accident. "Thanks for visiting to give me your good news in person, though."

Angelica didn't budge, even when I got up and gave her all the body language that said I was ready for her to go now. "What's wrong?"

"I don't know. I guess I'm jealous."

"Jealous? That's a good one." Snort. Angelica had a husband, and a baby coming, as the main ways she'd outdone me in life. Besides that, she had a posh mansion in the suburbs of the city. Brady made good money at his accounting firm, and she didn't even work unless she decided to do one of those home-sales-parties with purses or jewelry or candles with her rich wife friends now and then. "Jealous? Of what?"

"Never mind."

"No, come on. You can't just throw that out there."

"Candy Cane Cottage. It's like you stole that from me."

"Stole." I closed my eyes but lifted my eyebrows while I processed. Finally I opened them. "What are you talking about? I borrowed money and bought the building." I'd spent my childhood trying to be the family's representative gymnast in Angelica's stead. "That's a really strange take on it."

She broke into tears. "You could always do everything. I had to sit on the sidelines after my injury and do nothing but watch. While *I* was the one who wanted to train for the Olympics, you were the one getting the perfect tens. It killed me that you were so good and I just had to stare. You got to do everything that was meant for me to do."

More like I had to do everything in her place, like I was expected to live her life instead of mine. *Jeremy was right about me.* And I wasn't even up for explaining my side to Angelica. What good would it do? None while she was all emotional. Or while I was.

"Angelica, I am really sorry about that. I wish things had been different."

"Me, too." Finally, she left.

There was no time to process all that swirling information. I headed to the showcase. After so many years of running the Christmas extravaganza, despite the glitches of missing staff—meaning, Tennille—the assistants and I pulled through. The parents didn't even seem to notice that the wrong music played twice for the four-year-olds—firt "Rocking Around the Christmas Tree" and then "Feliz Navidad" instead of their assigned music, "Here Comes Santa Claus." To be fair, the four-year-olds hadn't notice, either. They just danced.

Moreover, the parents didn't know that we forgot a costume accessory addition—the hair bows for the seven-year-olds—and that we barely remembered the streamers in the back of the stage for the finale.

It worked out.

And if it hadn't, the parents would have achieved pretty much the same level of happiness at seeing their offspring springing on the mats.

When it finally ended, I worked at rolling up one of the mats. Most of the parents were gone, with just a few lingering near the door. I bent and pushed and wrestled the heavy foam.

Beside me, someone bent over to help me pull the mat out of the way. The cologne alerted me to his identity even before I could turn my head to see his chiseled jaw.

"Great show your gym put on."

"Jeremy? You were here?"

"I have tickets to the hockey game on Monday. It's here in town. Would you like to go?"

"I love hockey."

He nodded as if this was not news to him. He showed me the printed tickets. I saw the seats—very good seats—for the local farm team against the big time Reedsville Rhinos. "I'll see you then."

Was this a date?

Chapter 13

I wore a sweater, but I was still shivering. Jeremy sat on my non-bruised side, and he gave me his down vest, and then pressed an arm around me to keep me warm. We cheered for the Wilder River Lumberjacks for all we were worth. Jeremy's Pepsi sloshed out of the top of the cup during a big goal. It landed on my jeans. He took off his sweatshirt and used the sleeve to mop my pant-leg dry.

Without that sweatshirt, his t-shirt stretched across his muscles.

"You work out." It slipped out, I swear. I couldn't take my eye off the strain of the sleeve against his bicep. "Did you ever play sports?"

"Pitched for my unit's baseball team when I was in the military."

"Pitcher?" I was surprised. "You didn't play in high school, did you?"

"One of those late-discovered talents, I guess."

"I'm in favor of late discoveries."

"Good." Jeremy looked straight ahead as he said it, no grin or anything, but the crinkle at the side of his eye was an indication. "I'll hold you to that."

I wanted him to drop the *to that.* "With those biceps," I murmured.

"What was that?" he asked.

"What's that banner? Hooked on the edge of the rink. See it?" I pointed. "Houston Properties. Is that ... you?"

Jeremy gave a nonchalant shrug. "I like to support the local team."

I'd seen that banner a dozen times, but it'd never dawned on me it could be *Jeremy* Houston. "You sponsor a sports team."

He gave me a blank look, as if this should have been self-evident. "Tax write-off. Probably my most fun one."

"You sponsor other things, too?" I was catching on. "Like what? Never mind." I waved my hand. "I'm making you miss the match."

Later, believe me, I'd be looking up Houston Properties. Could Jeremy really own a business that sponsored teams? There'd been whispers, whispers that Jeremy had become highly successful, but I'd downsized them in my mind. Maybe ...

We ate nachos at the venue, but I was still hungry when the match ended, so Jeremy took me to dinner afterward. Wilder River didn't have a huge selection of restaurants in general, but there were fewer at that time of night. We drove out to the diner on the highway, where he ordered grilled cheese sandwiches and fries drizzled with ranch dressing for both of us—and he asked for mine to be cooked well-done.

"You know my favorite diner food?" I asked.

Again, with the knowing look. "It's everyone's favorite diner food. At least at Lou's Diner."

I couldn't argue with that. "Their cherry pie is good, too."

On the ride back to my house, Jeremy turned on the radio.

"You listen to The Aussie Boys?" I nearly lost my composure. "Jeremy. This is just too—" Creepy? No, wrong word. Coincidental?

"Whether you remember or not, you and I have spent a lot of time together."

Oh, that. "Darn it!" I let out an agonized wail. "Why can't I remember it?"

"If you did, I think you'd be glad."

But would he? "Would you be glad if I could remember it?"

He didn't answer. He pulled into my driveway, came around and helped me down from the truck. When he set me on my feet, he left his hands on my hips a little longer than necessary and stared into my eyes.

"You'd better go inside."

"You want to come in?"

"I'd better not."

"I'd like you to."

"Are you sure?"

I was sure. "As long as you remember that I'm a good girl."

"One of the many reasons I always liked you, Danica."

Past tense. It crushed me. We went inside. I invited him to sit down. "Wait there a second." I went to the kitchen and returned with a tall glass of ice and a can of Pepsi. I popped the top and poured it over the ice. We both watched as the foam rose and then fell. I poured in a little more and then handed it to him. "This is so you can focus."

"I see." He accepted it and took a sip. "What would you like me to focus on?"

"This." I took it from him and placed it on the table. I then knelt on the couch beside his hip and pressed a kiss to Jeremy's lips.

At first, he didn't react. At least not like I'd expected or hoped. It was more of a shocked inertia, with a hint of cola taste. "Are you sure?" he asked between our pressed lips.

"Mmm." I wrapped my arms around his neck and coaxed, teased, and practically begged him to respond. When he did, it was with a roar. The intensity of his kiss came from somewhere with temperatures similar to the center of the earth. Its heat singed my eyebrows. Its tenderness turned my skeletal system to pliant cartilage. His kiss left me limp, molten, and smoldering.

And dying for more. "That was good, Jeremy, but I think you might need a little more practice."

"Oh?" He pulled my hair back, exposing my ear and neck. "Do you know anyone who would volunteer to be my rehearsal partner?"

As his kiss passed over the spot below my ear, I exhaled with a soft moan—my version of volunteering for the next few minutes. Or it might have been hours. Or a million years. Jeremy's kiss was a time warp, all things present, past, and future in one. I could see forever in his eyes, and feel eternity as he held me.

"That drink really helped me focus." He traced a pattern on my forearm as I leaned against him. "I didn't think about anything besides kissing you that whole hour."

An hour? Wow. "Time flies when I'm kissing you. Which is what got us in trouble on the golf cart." I sat up straight. "Wait a second. I remember the golf cart." I whipped around to face him. "I remembered, Jeremy! I remembered the ..." ... the passionate make out that almost got us in trouble at the country club. "Wow." I placed my hand on my heating cheek. "We had a good time there."

"I see you actually do remember."

I bit my lips together. "Hmmm." That had been a good kiss. As good as this one tonight. "Jeremy, I can't believe I'd forgotten that. It was ... yeah. It was." It had been life-alteringly-good kissing him on the golf course. I hadn't even cared when Rufus called us out. "Oh, my gosh. I remember Rufus, too." Little bits—particles and chunks—were coming back to me.

I stood up and paced back and forth between the coffee table and the couch.

"You're getting more memories back?"

Here and there, flashes came. A ride in his truck, singing long and loud to The Aussie Boys. Cooking dinner together. That I'd promised to wash his truck. A fishing trip.

"Fishing wasn't our main activity on the fishing trip, was it?" A guilty grin tugged one side of my mouth. "But we saw the Perseids." I'd managed to stop kissing him long enough to appreciate the shooting stars. "Jeremy, we were close. Really close."

He reached for my hand and pulled me down onto his lap. "Yeah." He touched his forehead to mine. "You gave me a chance. Thanks."

"You gave me a chance, too." I kissed him softly once. "Can we"—I didn't know. Was it my place to ask this? *Can we give us a chance? Now?*

Jeremy pulled me into a hug. "It's been great."

159

I pulled out of the hug and looked at him. The verb tense of his statement bothered me. "What do you mean? *It's been* great."

"The past three months have been the best I can remember. At first, I thought I was taking a break from work, and coming to see if you could forgive me, but then everything happened."

"We happened," I corrected. "And are you—are you leaving again?"

He blinked once for yes, or so it seemed.

"Houston Properties?" My voice was dry, dusty-sounding. "You're needed back there." All those years, I'd rejected Jeremy for his incompetence and his bumbling dingbattiness. And now, come to find out, he was nothing like that. He helmed a purportedly huge business. He managed to get me out of a half dozen scrapes. He'd helped me heal. "But you left it for three months?"

"I did some distance work, now and then. But I have responsibilities that need to be completed in person."

He'd stayed in Wilder River that long time.

For me?

I shivered all over. "I get it. Your business is important." Really important. It did good things, too. "I'll miss you."

A war raged on his brow, as though he were trying to decide what to tell me next. He slid me off his lap and stood up. Finally, he turned to face me. "Danica. I'm the guy who ruined your sister's wedding."

Please. "I forgave you for that." It'd been an adolescent moment.

"You think I'm a screw-up."

"Are you?"

"No."

"Then I was wrong in the past." And I was going to let that go.

"Not entirely." He grimaced. "I did mess things up where you're concerned. A lot of things. Including something that happened while you had amnesia."

The air in the room thickened. "What do you mean?"

"I didn't tell you who I was when I came to visit you in the

160

hospital."

"You did tell me you were Jeremy Houston."

"Which meant nothing to you. At that point, you didn't even know your Great-Grandma Candalaria's name. I never explained that I was someone you despised."

This gave me pause. "You lied to me?"

He bit his lips together as my accusation skittered through the air.

"When I was incapacitated?" My pulse rate spiked. "Incapacitated, and you *knew* it?"

"I broke your trust." He stared at the floor. "I full-on admit I saw an opportunity and grasped it."

My head spun. I had fallen in love with him—but had I fallen in love with a lie? Or, worse, with a *liar?* "Jeremy." My voice quavered as I fought to keep my tone in check. "Why not tell me the truth and give me a chance to decide for myself?" Couldn't he have done me that courtesy?

"Because, Danica, I'd known you for years. I knew what you'd decide, if you were given the full facts. The whole town knew."

But—"No! I would've been rational! I would've weighed facts! And—"

No. The wind blew out of my lungs in a whoosh. He was absolutely correct: I would have suspected foul motives or pranks. In a heartbeat, I would have cast him out of the hospital room and never given him a chance. And yet—he'd *lied* to me! To win my trust, to win my *heart.*

Tears stung my eyes. "Jeremy, you do realize this makes you no better than Tennille and Liam, right?"

Everyone had taken advantage of me. Violated my trust while I was in a compromised mental state. Was there no one I could believe in anymore?

"You're upset." He looked like he'd swallowed a toad.

I cleared my throat to mask the emotion, but it came through anyway as my voice cracked. "You deceived me."

He scratched the side of his head, gave me a long stare, and then with a short nod said, "I'm sorry."

Jeremy brushed off his jeans, grabbed his parka from the hall tree, and gave me a sad wince from where he stood with his hand on the front door. "I never knew it would come to this. I really like you, but I also know you should never trust me."

And he was gone.

Chapter 14

Days passed, while I seethed. The more I pondered, the madder I got. Dr. Chen cleared me to drive, finally, and I fired up my car and drove to the valley overlook to think. Snow blanketed the whole world of Wilder River.

Jeremy done me seriously wrong!

Back home, I wrapped Christmas presents for each of the Candy Cane Cottage gymnasts, as well as for the coaches and assistants. But at our team party, I barely registered all the holiday cheer. Instead, I stood in the corner sipping hot chocolate from The Hot Chocolate Shoppe.

"You're brooding." My mom came and stood beside me with her cup of cocoa during the dance party portion of the event. She'd come to assist me at the party, since I'd lost Tennille and it was always good to have more adults on deck. "Is it because of Angelica's baby?"

"Of course not." Why would she say that? "I've got all the planning done for her baby shower, by the way—if you're still on board for doing it at your house."

"Naturally. Where else? Anyway, I just figured, you know, it's hard to see your sister move on to the next big milestone in life after you've had a breakup."

"That's for sure." And it reminded me I had plenty to do to get ready for the baby shower. "Jeremy and I weren't exactly dating, so it's not like we actually broke up. You hate Jeremy."

"True. He did ruin the biggest day of your sister's life with his stupid antics."

"Did he, though? Really, Mom?" *Ruined* was a strong word. Angelica had already gotten married. Jeremy had only rolled into the after-party on his motorbike. The vows had been the vital portion. "Do we have to keep dredging up the past with him? He's not that dorky boy anymore."

Now, he'd become a dorky, lying man.

The next day, I was still annoyed. Not just at Jeremy, though. In fact, I contacted several different friends, demanding to know what they'd thought when they'd seen me hanging out with Jeremy Houston, asking why they hadn't stopped me. Why they hadn't come up and slapped sense into me—or into him.

Everyone gave weak excuses.

My frustration grew.

But so did missing Jeremy. No matter how upset I'd been with him in the moment, I longed for him. It hurt that he'd lied, but did it hurt more that he left?

I was such a mess. It was a good thing gymnastics were done, and I could stick around home a lot and do things like make baby shower decorations—and not express my frustration in front of cute kids.

Snow fell. Liam and Tennille moved for real, but her much younger sister, Jocelyn King,—whom I'd always thought of as an apple who'd fallen *far* from the tree—signed on at Candy Cane Cottage as our business manager and whipped all of us into business shape. I had her to thank for the uptick in sales and the transformation of the place. I only had to show up and teach. It was the best. The kids were the best.

To pass the time while I brooded, I took gifts and groceries to Starlight Haven women's shelter over in Mendon, shoveled snow for every person on my block to work out my frustrations, and cleaned every cobweb from Mom's house to get the place spick and span for Angelica's next-biggest day of her life.

None of it rooted Jeremy out of my heart.

Had my bad reaction lost him to me forever? Which was worse—

his deception or my rejection of him?

I miss him. I've fallen for him. Should I forgive?

My heart knew the answer.

Sure, he might have pulled the wool over my already wooly eyes, but he'd saved Candy Cane Cottage from opportunistic so-called friends. He'd come for me when I wrecked my bike. He'd dressed my wounds. He'd taught me to cook. The texts showed truth—that he'd only appeared in my life when I requested him to. He'd been a perfect gentleman. A perfect boyfriend.

And I'd squandered it by getting mad over how things between us began.

But honestly! How else *could* they have begun? I'd been so doggedly blind to him! Only amnesia could have opened my eyes.

I needed him. In every way.

It'd been a full week without him, and I couldn't take another minute. I broke down and texted Jeremy. We needed to talk about it. He'd respond, and we'd talk it out, and everything would be fine! Hunky dory! We'd be together again by the holidays, and—

No reply.

Radio silence? Honestly, that was worse than getting a scathing message in return. *I really messed up.*

My sister Angelica came on the weekend to quilt with Mom. I went and helped stitch both a pink and a blue quilt with them, since Angelica and Brady had decided not to find out their baby's gender prior to the birth.

We finalized plans for the baby shower—the food, the games, the decorations. Baby! The world was all Christmas! All baby!

Except inside my own world. Mine went from dim to pitch dark. Without Jeremy, it was like when my collie, Lady, had died when I was nine years old. It shouldn't have felt like a death without a funeral, but it did. It almost made me wish my memories of falling in love with Jeremy Houston—twice—hadn't come back. Like, maybe I should hit my head again and they'd selectively delete.

I ran into Garrett Bolton at the grocery store. Mom would hate me for squandering an opportunity to flirt with him, but instead I asked about his cousin. Loser move of me.

"Have you heard from Jeremy? It's been weeks." And then, the dam burst. Right there in front of the boxed brownie mix display, a place that should have given me comfort. Instead, I emitted a sniffling, disgusting, donkey-cry. Talk about loser moves!

"Hey, Danica." Garrett left his cart near me, and disappeared for a few seconds, only to return with a stack of napkins from the deli. "You're okay. It's going to be okay."

More like I was creating a scene. People heard me and steered their carts away from the frosting and birthday candles aisle. "Jeremy ghosted me."

"That's not like him." He handed me a napkin. "Other guys, maybe, but not Jeremy."

"I know, right?" I sniffled, and tears fell hot. I wiped them until the napkin soaked. "He's usually so considerate. He's just the greatest, Garrett, and I lost him."

"Maybe he's out of cell range." He handed me another napkin.

"Nowhere on earth is out of cell range." I could have stomped my foot, but then I remembered he was in the Army Reserve and might have to do his two-week camp, so there was a chance he could be out of cell range. "What should I do?"

"You actually like him." Garrett looked dubious. "He ruined Angelica's wedding. He tricked you while you had that memory loss. Everyone knows you can't forgive him."

"Everyone?" Jeremy had talked to Garrett about me at some point since I unintentionally booted him from my life, it was clear. "Garrett. What do you know?" I could have grabbed him by the collar and shaken the details from him.

Unfortunately, Garrett was Fort Knox. "I'm his family. I can't betray his trust. Family is family."

I wished I could be Jeremy's family, too, though. Not that Jeremy would believe that at this point, not after how badly I'd reacted. "You're good at this comforting thing."

"My wife used to say so."

Wife. Oh, right. He'd been married at one time. I sniffled hard. "At least tell me one thing—Jeremy's favorite meal."

"Uh, Danica. You don't cook."

"How would you know that?"

"You and I had culinary class together in high school. Until they reassigned you to sewing class."

"It was wood shop."

"My point stands." Garrett's posture fell. "Fine. He loves traditional holiday dinners like ham and rolls and mashed potatoes and gravy. He likes a really good dessert thing his mom used to make, but I have no idea how you'd get that recipe."

"What was in the dessert?"

"Jell-o, maybe? It was good, I know that."

So, not jell-o? "Please don't say jell-o with shredded carrots and diced pears."

"Gross. No, I think it was strawberries and pretzels."

"I think I know what you're talking about!" My spirits sang. Jeremy had made that for me once. It'd been in my refrigerator after I regained my memories the first time.

Garrett huffed a sigh. "They may say that the way to a man's heart is through his stomach, but in your case, Danica, I'd go a different route. What about getting a slinky dress and a pair of heels? Or maybe writing him a nice poem?"

All good suggestions. "Does he like poetry?" He did read me *Jane Eyre*. I'd write a gothic novel if I had to. I'd pull out all the stops.

"He likes Pepsi."

I'd write a poem about Pepsi. "Thanks!" For the first time in ages, I could see a glimmer of light. "Can you tell me the best way to reach him?"

Garrett gave me a tip. I resolved to act on it—as soon as possible.

Chapter 15

The Candy Cane Cottage buzzed with activity. Two days until Christmas, and the gymnastics room had been transformed into Christmas baby shower central. Dad had even gone to the lengths of setting up a full kitchen in one corner of the room and hauling in a half dozen sofas and recliners for guests, plus dozens of folding chairs. It was almost as elaborate as Angelica's wedding reception, when they'd transformed the back yard.

"You have got to be kidding me." Angelica placed a hand on her growing belly. "I'll go into labor if you bring that man to my baby shower."

"Don't be dramatic." I placed the final stitches on the binding of the pink quilt. The blue one was already finished. All my years of making costumes with Tennille had not been in vain. "He's not the guy we thought he was."

"If he rides a motorcycle here, I'm going to slash his tires."

"Angelica?" Mom intervened. "Is it better to put one brazil nut or two in each nut cup at the place settings? Back in my day, only women and girls came to baby showers. Adding men to the mix, we might as well just call it a party."

Was this Mom's way of saying she didn't want Jeremy there either?

"You'll both like the man I'm bringing to the party, I promise."

"What I don't like is the veritable half-ton of flour that went to waste while you learned to make homemade rolls." Mom waved her hand in front of her face, as if to swat away floating motes of flour dust. "Why can't you buy them from the bakery like the rest of us?"

"Or use the frozen dough?" Angelica asked. "Brady doesn't know the difference. Just a slight deception. Like wearing makeup while you're dating. Or pretending you like watching hockey."

"I do like hockey."

"You would." Angelica helped me fold the finished quilt. "I'll admit, though, the rolls do taste good." She grabbed for one from beneath the tinfoil cover. "Is there real butter in the recipe? Whose recipe is it?"

Jeremy's mom's. As well as the recipe for the strawberry jell-o with cream cheese and pretzels. After a lot of cajoling, Garrett had given me her number, and I'd bitten the bullet and called her. *Please let my dessert be up to par.*

Dad came in, as well as a few guests. We set up the rest of the buffet on the long tables draped with Christmas plaid tablecloths. More guests arrived. Angelica's husband brought his parents and two younger sisters. Instrumental Christmas music played in the background. We had wassail simmering on the stove, and a ham in the oven to create an olfactory heaven. The gym's biggest Christmas tree had been taken over by the baby shower, and instead of traditional glass bulb ornaments, it was all baby hands and feet created from painted tiles and hanging from burlap strings.

Just two days until Christmas—and I still didn't know whether Jeremy had received my message. Whether or not he'd come. Whether or not he was legitimately ghosting me.

Whether I stood a Christmas miracle of a chance with him.

"Wow. Nice spread," Brady's dad said, entering from the parking lot, stomping off his boots, and taking a deep breath. "Smells like holiday heaven."

"Our family loves ham," the taller of the teenage sisters said. "We put little cloves in it like they taught us in culinary class at school." She sniffed it. "Is that where you learned to make a ham?" she asked me. "It smells like cloves."

It wasn't clear if she loved or hated cloves. We talked culinary, and I admitted I'd been ejected from that class. She thought I was kidding. "You're funny. You should date my older cousin."

"Thanks, but my heart is already spoken for." I glanced at the large wall clock—still no Jeremy! The party was set to start any second.

"Is he coming today?" she asked.

"Probably?" My voice had a tremble. I'd mailed the letter to the address Garrett gave me. Since then, I'd gotten no reply, no texts, nothing. All this might be in vain.

But I hoped it wasn't. I wanted my vision of his return to me to be real so much—it just had to happen.

"We'd better get started before the food gets cold." Dad clapped for everyone's attention. The three dozen or so guests gathered around the buffet tables, eyeing the food I'd made especially for Jeremy and which had ignored Angelica's demand that we have The Hot Chocolate Shoppe cater it with their roast beef paninis, grilled mushrooms and onions, and the herbed olive oil.

I hope he comes to eat it.

"We'd like to thank Danica for this meal and for creating this party to celebrate Angelica's and Brady's upcoming life change, and to celebrate Angelica making Nancy and me grandparents." There was some laughter, but not from me. With every passing minute, my heart sank more. "We're also doubly grateful for Danica's health returning after her accident this past summer—as it seems to have jarred loose in her brain the locked door to her cooking skills."

More chuckles. Someone patted me on the back. Angelica gave a little huff.

"Angelica, we're so happy for your baby, and ..." Dad droned on. Mom looked impatient.

I was dying slowly inside. Jeremy hadn't come. I'd made all this food for him, invited him the only way I could, and even prepared all the supplies—a bucket of hot water, a special huge sponge, a chamois, and a ladder—so I could finally make good on my promise to wash his truck, no matter the weather outside.

I owed him that. And so much more.

And my dad was going on. And on. And on. About Angelica.

Outside, a loud engine revved. Loudly.

"Is that a motorcycle?" Angelica shrieked. "I said if there was a motorcycle I'd go into labor."

I ran to the back door, pressing my face against the little square of glass that served as a window. There, in the snow, was a motorbike with a big man astride it. The bike pulled a wagon of some fashion—and in the wagon was a strangely shaped protrusion. I pushed the door open.

"Hi." Jeremy lifted his helmet off and exposed a grin. "Can you help me with my baby shower gift?" He pointed to the tarp-covered, pointy-looking thing in the sidecar. "It's heavier than I expected, and as you might remember, I'm not the best motorcycle driver even when it's *not* snowy."

Underneath the tarp lay an enormous ice sculpture.

"It's ... a stork." I stared.

"Better than a swan, you know, for this occasion."

"Is this to make up for the swan?" That swan still floated head-down in my parents' pool in my mind's eye.

"A swan is a terrible thing to waste." His eye twinkled. "But you have to admit, the thing was so beautifully carved that it likely had a soul that had yearned to fly free."

"That is so true." I stared at the stork, its beak holding a delicately carved knot of a baby blanket, with a baby's face poking out from below the chin. "When you hit it with your motorcycle, it briefly did fly free."

Together, we hefted it from its sidecar nest and took it into the makeshift kitchen, where we quickly cleared a spot at the center of the buffet table, wedging it between the relish tray and the mashed potatoes.

The crowd quit talking and stared at the ice sculpture. And at Jeremy.

"Jeremy Houston?" someone whispered, in mock horror. Or possibly real horror.

"Danica!" Mom hissed. "You promised."

"How do you like the ice sculpture?" I asked the crowd. "Well played, Jeremy. Right? Everyone?"

He didn't seem the least bit cowed by the cold reception. "I thought a stork was fitting, considering that I ruined a bird at the last big party for Angelica." This earned him a laugh, and the party's chatter resumed. Some even clapped. One person cheered for the stork.

Mom distracted herself with food. But she thawed when Jeremy complimented her on the beauty of her daughters and congratulated her on the impending grandchild. That got her smiling at last.

Finally, Angelica said, "Thanks for the bird. You've made restitution. Let's eat." Everyone lined up at the buffet, resumed talking about the baby, and no one seemed to mind that Jeremy—all grown up and successful thanks to Pepsi—was there with us. With *me*.

Whew.

In the crazy new-normalness of it all, Jeremy smiled down at me. "Are you finally impressed?"

"Impressed with one of your pranks?"

"With my grand gesture, I should say."

"It's truly grand. You can tell your sister Penelope I'm impressed. And that her advice was sound."

"Yeah?" He broke into a grin. "Finally!"

"And while you're telling people things, you can tell me I'm an idiot." It was time to apologize—hard core.

"You are?" He pulled back and chuckled.

"For letting myself get upset—when all you'd done since my accident was help me. All you'd done was be the best friend and confidant and boyfriend and support I could've asked for." He'd even taken me home from the hospital, when my parents hadn't been there, due to their trip. "I was rash in my reaction, and an idiot. Hundred percent. I should be the one bringing *you* a large carved-ice stork, not

172

the other way around."

"I can think of a better grand gesture, to be honest." He kissed me softly—in front of everyone.

Truly grand, that kiss.

My mom gasped. "Jeremy Houston! Danica! What are you doing?"

I was kissing Jeremy—even before I'd taken time to introduce him to my family anew. "I made you some dinner," I said to Jeremy, ignoring Mom. "That's one facet of my grand gesture."

"I like it! The kiss is excellent as well." He kissed my forehead, took his gaze off me and looked at the buffet. "Ham and rolls? And mashed potatoes? You made all of it? How did you know that was my favorite?"

For once, I was the one to give the enigmatic lift of the eyebrow. "There wasn't room on the counter for dessert yet. It's in here." I led him by the hand to the bank of three fridges Dad had rented for the event, where the five large pans of his mother's recipe waited. "Do you recognize it?"

"I recognize sweet things when I see them." Away from everyone's eyes, Jeremy kissed me solidly. "When I got back in the country last night after my Reserve duties, my phone received a barrage of texts akin to Hurricane Sandy. Most of them were about business. I skipped all of them but yours. Then, at home, I saw your invitation with the date and time for this shindig. Sorry I was late. I booked the ice sculptor last minute. And I had to buy a motorcycle. You'd be surprised how hard it is to find a sidecar."

"Sidecar?" Oh, for the stork to ride in!

Wow. He'd bought a motorcycle. For this. For me. Just to make this day hilariously perfect. "The stork is awesome." Jeremy was awesome. "I'm really sorry I didn't react well to your *Grease 2* homage back in the day." Or to any of the other gestures. "I wish I'd seen you for what you are."

Jeremy took my hand, and we left the buffet and the party and Angelica's worshipers. Out back, in the moonlight, we stood and watched the snow fall. The same moonlight we'd kissed in while fishing so many weeks ago.

"I have to tell you something," I said.

"Something good or bad?" he asked.

"My memories of our time together returned in full." They'd come piecemeal over the weeks since Jeremy left, each one accompanied by a stabbing pain. "When you didn't answer my calls, I thought I'd lost you."

Jeremy squeezed my hand. "When you didn't call for a few days, I hoped I hadn't lost you." He explained about his military assignment, winter camp for Army Reserve, how it'd been in an isolated area, said he'd missed me—wished things had gone differently. "I spent the whole winter camp kicking myself for lying to you."

"In retrospect, I know you didn't lie. You just gave me the truth in small doses. Like I say, my memories of our time together did come back. All of them." Including the sweeping, amazing falling-in-love moments. The ones that made my soul soar now.

"Well, forgive me for making you think I'd ghosted you," he said, pressing my hand and looking down at me with something like pain in his eyes. "Garrett told me he saw you in the grocery store."

"Did he tell you about the stack of napkins?" I grimaced. "It was a twelve-napkin meltdown."

"Thanks to the dozen deli napkins, I knew you were ready for me to come back." He kissed the top of my head and wrapped an arm around my waist. I rested my head on his shoulder. "It's good to be home at Christmas."

"Home is where the heart is." I turned to him and wrapped my arms around his waist. "Your heart has a home in my heart, Jeremy."

Wherever I went in this life from now on, I wanted it to be with Jeremy. Jeremy was my home.

On the back lot of Candy Cane Cottage in the softly falling snow, Jeremy kissed me again. "Let's remember how this moment feels." He kissed me again. "For all the Christmases to come."

Chapter 16

A Year Later

"Come on in!" Mom held wide the door to Candy Cane Cottage and waved Jeremy and me inside. "It's so cold out here. Oh, and look at how you're walking. You look like a penguin."

Mom always knew just what to say. "It's getting close now." I patted my rounding belly. "It's exciting that Angelica's daughter and mine will only be a year apart in age. Cousins that can grow up together."

"That's only if you live near each other." Mom took the pile of presents from my arms, gifts that had been mailed to Jeremy's and my home in Reedsville and which we had decided to bring to the baby shower in the snowy mountains of Wilder River. "Since Angelica and Brady moved back to Wilder River, you'll have to make an effort. A real effort."

"Mom." I hugged her, once both our arms were free, with the presents piled on the long table near the check-in desk of the gym. "I know it's been bothering you that I decided to move to Reedsville after Jeremy's and my wedding at Valentine's Day." We hadn't waited long to tie the knot. With a long history like ours, there was no need to delay to get to know each other better. "But he's the one with the established business."

"You're saying Candy Cane Cottage isn't an established business?" She waved an arm around the room, a space that had improved greatly while in Jocelyn King's stewardship. It was no stretch for me to say she'd doubled my revenues, and she'd made the interior so much more cheery and homey. I could imagine this becoming a pre-school, or even a K-8. But only if we lived in Wilder River. Which we didn't. Which we wouldn't.

I was finished mourning about my loss of Candy Cane Cottage. I had let it go emotionally during the first six weeks after my relocation to Reedsville. Like I told Mom, it only made sense to live where Jeremy worked. But walking back inside, feeling the connection to Grandma, with my heart reigniting all the happy shrieks of kids who were learning their somersaults and winter-peppers—I soaked up the nostalgia, and I did feel a little sad.

"Mrs. Houston! You're here!" Jocelyn came and took me by both hands. "Would you like a tour of the improvements?" She whisked me through the rooms, pointing out little upgrades. "I hope it's okay. I had a few free hours in the evenings, and I've just got too much nervous energy to ever really sit down, and isn't TV the worst? And I could never read a book. Well, except those books Garrett writes."

"Garrett?" I asked, but she was off again, pointing out the wainscoting, the new sink she'd installed in the girls' restroom, drawing out her plans for a kitchenette. "You're pretty amazing, Jocelyn."

"I'm running out of things to do in here is the only problem. It scares me that I could get bored. I heard the Hot Chocolate Shoppe has been sold to someone who knows nothing about running a small business in a tiny town. What if they don't know the recipe for the roast beef panini sandwiches? What if they use the wrong cheese and don't add provolone? Those are a town tradition! Do you think I should offer them my services? Work there part-time? Probably not. I don't want to divide my attention, when you need me here and I owe you my first loyalty." She squeezed my hand and then rushed off to greet some of the gymnastics families who had come for the baby shower. They had a show for me, apparently, and Jocelyn needed to get everything ready.

"She's a wonder." Angelica looped her arm through mine. "Have you seen? India's walking already. She walks better than I do." She patted her hip. "I hope she always does. Maybe she can do gymnastics here at Candy Cane Cottage."

"Too bad my Jane won't get to."

Jane. That's the name Jeremy had insisted on, considering the fact Jane Eyre had brought the two of us together. It was sweet of him.

Jane Candalaria Houston, in honor of both my great-grandmother and me.

Angelica went on talking about India, who, in Angelica's eyes, was likely to rule the world. Meanwhile, I peered around the room for Jeremy. He stood talking to his cousin Garrett Bolton. Could he be the Garrett with books that Jocelyn mentioned? Nah, Garrett Bolton worked at the plant, and he had for years. Well, other than the few years he'd moved to college and married that woman. What had her name been? Well, anyway, they'd been in that car accident, and she'd died. Sometimes I forgot he'd ever left Wilder River. He was such a fixture.

We talked about India for a while, and I glanced around the room until I spied Jeremy. He stood talking to Garrett. I shuffled that direction. Waddled, more like. Angelica stayed at my side, continuing to talk about India. Admittedly, my niece was one of the cutest babies alive, so the topic was welcome. But ever since moving away from Wilder River, I'd come to see that Jeremy had been right—the Denton family revolved around Angelica.

The past year had been radically different—with Jeremy's whole world revolving around me. And soon, both our orbits would circle Jane.

Jane kicked. I rested a hand on my belly.

As I came up to Jeremy's side, I caught snippets of his conversation with Garrett over the sound system's rendition of "Rockin' Around the Christmas Tree."

"You won't guess what I brought as a gift for your baby." Garrett pushed a gift bag into Jeremy's hands. "Go ahead, open it."

"It's not time to open presents. And isn't the mother-to-be supposed to open them?" Jeremy pushed it back into Garrett's grasp. "No spoilers."

"Spoiler—it's a Wilder River Wolves cheerleading uniform. A tiny one."

"But what if our daughter doesn't want to be a cheerleader?"

"She will be the best gymnast. They'll practically force her to join the cheer squad. This is just to prep her mentally for the task. Mental prep is half the battle, you know."

"Garrett, you forget." I accepted the gift bag, giving a nod of thanks. "We don't even live in Wilder River. Our kids will be going to some gigantic high school in Reedsville where they won't know half their classmates' names. Or even a tenth of them."

"About that, Danica." Jeremy took my hand and led me to the door. "Can we talk?"

Before I could protest, he had led me out the back door and into the parking lot where I'd seen him hiding in the bushes last year after he'd door-ditched the giant vase of flowers.

"What is going on, Jeremy?"

"I didn't want to tell you until gift-opening time, but on second thought, it's probably better to tell you in private, rather than in front of everyone."

My stomach quivered, and not from baby Jane's kicks. "What are you telling me, Jeremy?"

"Remember when I made the trip to Wilder River without you last month?"

"Um, yeah?" My stomach now housed a jackhammer. "Is there something I should know? You said you were looking at commercial property."

"I was. For us. For Houston Properties. To build its headquarters here in Wilder River."

178

"Jeremy!"

"I know, it's something we should have discussed together, but would you oppose relocating from Reedsville back here? So we can raise Jane near our families, and so you can run Candy Cane Cottage yourself?"

"Would I oppose it!" I gasped, throwing my arms around him. "It would be my dream!" Something snapped in my belly. Something different—and a little scary. "Jeremy?" My focus wrenched wildly away from our future and to the immediate present. "I think you'd better get me to the hospital."

"Wilder River doesn't have an obstetrics department." Jeremy scooped me into his arms and started running for his truck.

"I don't care—I don't care if the janitor is the only person there. I am having this baby. Now."

***

Three hours later, and after several chapters of *Jane Eyre* read aloud to calm me, I gave the final push.

"Congratulations, Mrs. Houston." Dr. Haught, the attending physician who was only visiting during the final bit of his medical training, held our little girl in his arms, and a nurse came over with a clean towel, rubbed Jane all over, and then set baby girl on my chest. "You have a healthy baby girl."

My heart might split wide open. "I can't believe it. She was born right here in Wilder River." I gazed down at her ruddy little squinched cheeks—the most beautiful baby in the whole world. "Jeremy?" I looked up for him, and he looked at me with so much love. "We started the last chapter of our lives together in a hospital room. And this is the next."

He pushed the hair off my forehead and leaned over to kiss me. "I'll never forget this moment. Together."

Epilogue

Roxanna

I had to get this right. Even in the freezing cold, with bare feet on this snowfield. Even though it was something as dumb in real life as making my hair swing in a flat swish, for my job today, it had to be perfect.

I have to be perfect.

"More snap on this take, please, Sanna." Domingo snapped his Spaniard fingers at me to demonstrate. "More twist at the last second, slow and then fast."

"Right." I gave him the go-ahead to roll the camera again. Then, I set my signature enigmatic smile, widened my eyes as much as possible, and swung my waist-length hair.

"That's it." Domingo lowered his camera and gave me one of those marveling looks that I'd grown used to. "Two takes. Wow. They said you were the best, but I wasn't prepared for two takes."

It should've been one.

"Tell me what you need, and I'll do my best to get it on the first try next time." The legendary Fred Astaire prepared for every shoot so it could be done with one take. Fred was my idol.

Someday, if I ever get time, I'd love to watch the scene of Fred tap dancing in the spinning room with someone I love.

At this rate, though—with my shooting schedule for Gloss and the scramble for my master's degree—I'd never have time for dating.

Domingo's assistant called to the group. "We're out of light so we'll wrap for the evening, but we will start first thing in the morning."

Just prior to sunrise. When the light was best—or right after sundown but before dark. That way, the hazy glow of natural twilight could work its lighting magic without shadows.

Ah, the working hours of my job.

Bitsy raced over to me and placed a warm, fuzzy red blanket over my shoulders. "You were great, Sanna."

"Yes, you were." Domingo packed up his camera. "You impressed me with your professionalism." His eyes twinkled above his gray beard, like a snow field sparkling on a sunny day. "You're going places, young lady."

I couldn't suppress a broad, grateful smile. A tired one. This had been a long day—starting long before pre-dawn light, while hair and makeup staff had transformed me into Sanna.

"Yes, she is." Bitsy hugged me. "Like, back to her room to take a hot bath to be ready for tomorrow." She shuffled me toward the Wilder River Lodge, where I was staying for the week. "He liked that you're such a pro. A word from Domingo could lead to bigger and better jobs, you know. In movies and TV."

Maybe, and it sounded like a dream, but it wasn't the job I wanted. Hair modeling was the most fun I'd ever had, but I needed to focus on my bigger goal—getting that master's degree in English literature pinned down.

"I'm now and always a still-photos model, not an actress." I slipped my feet into the snow boots Bitsy had set out. Heavenly—so warm! "But thanks for your confidence in me."

"You could do anything, I'm sure, Sanna. Why are you back in school?" Bitsy asked this all the time.

"You of all people should know that a job in the modeling business only lasts so long, unless you're a mega-star first like"—I named a few hair- or skin-care models who'd come into the endorsement business after successful television and movie careers. "I'm getting my master's for *after* my Sanna star burns out."

Well, that was only partly true. Having a long-term modeling career would be wonderful. So would acting. I felt so alive in front of the camera. But that was the thing—my life wasn't the right thing to focus on.

Mom's was.

"But you can earn more and more commissions. Just be wise with your income and you can probably retire in five years." Bitsy, as my agent, knew exactly what I earned. But that wasn't the point.

"I like being prepared." Besides, the income had all turned to outgo lately, thanks to Thorn Atkin, my nemesis.

"That is your motto. Always prepared. Like Domingo said, full of professionalism." She laughed. "I think he could have used *perfectionism* instead."

"Normally, that's a hundred percent true." We arrived at the back entrance of the Wilder River Lodge, where I'd be staying for the night. River Tresses was putting me up in the nicest suite with an amazing view of the ski slope-covered mountainside. "But I'm supposed to be going to a local book club tonight, and I'm actually *not* prepared."

"What do you mean, prepared? Are they asking you to speak about your career? Is it a nonfiction-about-careers book group?"

Hardly. "It's something I have to do for grad school. A requirement." For reasons too annoying to explain, I was locked into attending Twelve Slays of Christmas, hosted by Wilder River's Hot Chocolate Shop.

"And you're not prepared? As in …?"

"As in, I'"—I winced—"I haven't read the book yet." I shut my eyes and covered my face with my freezing cold hands.

A gasp. "Roxanna! You?" Bitsy stutter-stepped as we reached the outer doors of the lodge. "That's unthinkable!"

Right? "Well, I intend to be totally prepared—by seven o'clock." I looked at the giant clock near the ski-rental door of the resort. "I have three hours. Better crack the spine of the book."

Bitsy shook her head. "You're going to have to read fast."

I hustled to my room and found the copy of Agatha Christie's novel, *Sparkling Cyanide.*

Crime novels. My shoulders bunched. Give me fantasy, sci-fi, historical fiction, biography—all the books. But not crime fiction.

For so many reasons.

I winced as I cracked the spine for the tenth time.

And promptly fell asleep.

My alarm beeped at six thirty—telling me my ride would be downstairs in fifteen minutes to take me to the book group—and I shot up in bed. My heart pounded, and I started hyperventilating.

I shot around the hotel room. There was no time to put my contacts back in. I'd have to wear my thick glasses. My hair looked like ten rats had spent the entirety of my nap turning it into their tangled nest. My makeup was smeared to kingdom come.

With enough vigorous friction to nearly remove skin, I scrubbed my face makeup-free. Otherwise, I'd get arrested for impersonating that creepy clown with the balloon. The alarm beeped again. Five minutes to Danica's arrival.

Danica, my oldest friend, and my ride to the Hot Chocolate Shop, was the one person in Wilder River who knew my job status. I'd mentioned that to Bitsy, who'd warned that since I'd already told Danica it was fine—but that it had better not go an inch farther.

Unfortunately I was still only a few pages into the Agatha Christie novel! There wasn't even time to read the Cliff's Notes version of it! I could look up the Wikipedia summary.

That was my only hope.

Oh, mercy. Where was a hat? I dug around in my bag and found something! Aha! A beanie. Baby pink, and not my color, but I shoved my signature waves of dark hair up into it.

How lumpy was it? I leaned toward the mirror, stuffing a stray lock back inside it and—

Oh, no. The beanie was not only baby pink, it had a cat's face embroidered on it, a gift I'd planned on giving mama-to-be Danica to match the one I had for her baby daughter—with coordinating pink sweaters. Mother-daughter sweaters and beanies. So cute—in theory.

Oh, and let's not ignore the cat ears pointing at the top.

A lumpy cat-head atop my own head.

And I hadn't read the book.

Eighty percent of me whined like a cat in a rainstorm, saying, *Just forget the book club for tonight! Try again another week!* But the stern, logical twenty percent of me shoved her hands on her hips and said, *Suck it up, Dixie cup, and get over there. You have a full twelve of these suckers to attend, whether you like mystery novels or not, or else you can kiss your master's thesis goodbye.*

Fine. Fine! I shoved that stray snarl back into the hat and grabbed the unread book and headed downstairs.

Glowingly pregnant Danica stomped on the brake as we reached a stop sign. "You didn't read the book?" Her jaw dropped, her eyes widening. "And you're still attending the club? You do know the discussion is being led by Freya, right?"

Winter wind whipped, echoing Danica's horror.

"It's my first time attending. Won't she be lenient?" Ugh, I hated asking for favors, but this book club, Twelve Slays of Christmas, was my one and only option—ugh. No, thanks, murder mysteries and police and detectives. "You said Wilder River was full of really nice people."

"It's Freya," Danica repeated, as if that explained everything. "If you don't read the book, you're kicked out of the club. I tried joining last spring, during Freya's Spring into Reading session, but I couldn't keep up, thanks to a double enrollment of gymnasts at Candy Cane Cottage."

"And?"

"And she didn't give second chances."

Ooh. That didn't bode well.

But—but what choice did I have? It was this or the Russian Literature and Latte group that met weekly in Reedsville. Which would be fine if I weren't working and could read massive tomes all day and night between club meetings.

I leaned my head against the window. One of the cat ears bent, poking into my scalp. I sat up. "What should I do?"

"I don't know, Roxanna. But your hat is cute."

"It's actually for you, and I bought one for your baby."

"It's adorable." Danica rubbed her forehead and pointed across the parking lot to my destination. "You're shivering. Are you cold?"

I was chilled to the bone, despite my cozy nap. From my bag containing Agatha's book, I pulled out the cat sweater and put it on with an apologetic wince. "I bought this for you, to go with the kitty hat."

"It's darling. Meow. You match." She snorted. We pulled into a parking lot with a few cars in it. In front of a cozy-looking building, a large wooden sign read, The Hot Chocolate Shop. "See that truck over there?"

I saw it. An old white truck with yard tool handles sticking up at odd angles from its bed was parked beneath a towering evergreen.

"It belongs to Jeremy's cousin Grant Calhoun."

"That's nice." Wait a second. "I'm not interested in meeting anyone right now."

"He's your type."

I doubted that highly. "I have yet to meet *my type.*"

"Then what *is* your type?"

Humph. "I'll know it when I see it." I'd never had time to define it, not since I was too young to know myself well enough. So far, my adult years' experience with men had been wholly disappointing. Okay, that was solely based on Dad's world-shattering lie, but still.

"Well, you'll see your type when you meet him. Girl, he's everybody's type. And not just based on his looks."

"I doubt that."

"Trust me, you'll change your mind."

No, I wouldn't. I had a degree to earn, a long-lost dream to accomplish. And a bloodsucking attorney's fees to repay. Much as I wished for it, it was out of the question right now.

"Thanks for the ride and the advice." I gripped Agatha to my chest. "I'll be polite to Jeremy's cousin if I meet him, I promise."

"Good luck with Freya." Danica pulled a scared face. "I can pick you up later. Bye."

I climbed out, and she drove off.

The Hot Chocolate Shop, with its warm glowing windows, its lone pine tree out front and its soft Christmas-red paint looked welcoming, like Christmas in a box—at least from the outside.

Might as well face Freya and my fate. Someone who owned a place so welcoming had to be forgiving, right?

With a shudder, I climbed the steps to the shop. If I hadn't needed to cover my hair-nest, I would have shaken it out, squared my shoulders, and stalked inside, ready for anything.

Unfortunately, I sported dumb little cat ears, *plus* the fuzzy sweater for Danica. It had two white cats on the front. With the words *Jingle Cats* embroidered on it.

It had looked so cute in the shop when I'd been shooting on location in Japan last year! Now, it just seemed dumb, unless Danica was wearing it and matching her baby.

But I wasn't Danica. And there were no babies on my horizon, more's the pity.

The door jingled, and I entered a heavenly scented room. Chocolate essence swirled in the air all around, as well as warm spices like cinnamon and nutmeg and cloves. Mugs of all sizes and shapes hung from hooks along a peg board behind the counter. A large glass case contained a display of sandwiches under glass domes that made my mouth water, all on little stoneware plates of different designs. A huge fireplace stood against one side, with chairs and couches nearby, and a fire blazed and crackled.

Wow, talk about a reader's paradise!

"Welcome." A woman stood behind a counter spread with silver kettles. She wore an apron with the name *Freya* embroidered across the front. "Are you here for Twelve Slays?"

"Yes, I'm Roxanna Reid."

Freya checked a list and then looked back at me with narrowed eyes. "So, did you?"

"I'm sorry. *So, did I* what?" I accepted a mug of steaming hot chocolate from her hands. It smelled faintly of almonds. Cute, considering today's club focused on poisoning by cyanide, which smells of almonds.

"Did you read?"

Oh, a pun on my name, Roxanna Reid. Yikes. The moment of truth had attacked much sooner than expected. What to do? Lie? Fall at her feet and beg for mercy? I couldn't.

"Since you're hesitating"—Freya's warm smile faded, and she reached for my mug to take it back—"I'm guessing you didn't."

I gave Freya back the mug, but before we could finalize my dismissal, someone piped up.

"Honesty is the best policy." A man's voice sailed through the air from near the fire.

I walked over to see who had interjected his comment into our conversation. Over a pair of dark-rimmed glasses a young man with an intelligent aura eyed me.

"Full disclosure, I didn't read the book. No valid excuses either." Something about him made me add a flirtation to my voice. "Did you? Read, that is?"

"I take it you like cats."

Cats! Oh, right. The beanie and sweater. "You didn't answer my question."

"You didn't answer mine."

"You didn't ask me a question."

"Yes, I did. I asked if you liked cats."

"No, you asserted your assumption. It's not the same thing. Did you read the book?"

"No, but unlike you, I do have a valid excuse." He lowered the book he was reading—one twice as thick as the murder mystery we'd been assigned for the evening's club—and with a cover and title I recognized. "An excellent one, in fact."

"Oh, yeah?" Excuses bugged me. I rejected them in my own life, and others ought to as well.

"Yep." The guy stood up. He towered over me. At his full height, the breadth of his shoulders became wow-level impressive. If my manager ever saw this guy, she'd ask about signing him to a contract in a hot second.

Speaking of hot, was I standing too close to the hearth? The guy continued to stare me down. It had to be the blazing fireplace. Because I didn't react to ogling men.

Occupational hazard I'd learned to ignore.

Excepting now, apparently.

I resisted the urge to fan myself.

He's only ogling your weird cat ears and sweater. Not the same as when men gaped while I was a hundred percent hair and makeup, looking like Sanna, the ubiquitous face of Gloss hair products. Right now, I was a cat lady with glasses and lame excuses.

I gathered up my scattered bits of dignity. "I take it you're going to tell me your excuse, er—?"

This must be Jeremy's cousin. The guy with the truck.

Girl, he's everybody's type. And not just based on his looks.

I had major life struggles to focus on right now—regardless of any action-hero magnetism in a hot-nerd package.

"Go ahead. Tell me your excuse." I stood a little closer to him than necessary. "Grant Calhoun." The name rolled across my tongue like a delicious piece of chocolate.

"My reputation precedes me?" He extended his hand.

"My friend Danica dropped me off and pointed out your truck. Said you'd be in here."

"Ah. She's great. Glad she married Jeremy. He deserved her." He reached to shake my hand. When our hands touched, and my brain emptied, like a can of marbles dumped upside down. "I'm pleased to meet you."

"I'm Roxanna Didn't Read." My voice went scratchy.

He chuckled and simply disconnected our clasp—as if Mr. Eleven-on-a-Ten-Scale hadn't felt any of that electrifying zap.

Dang!

"My excuse is that I'm not a member of Twelve Slays of Christmas book club. I'm just here to drink Freya's excellent hot chocolate. She owns the shop."

"That is a proper excuse," I reluctantly admitted. The extension cord from whatever source had been lighting me up unplugged. My voice probably sounded dejected.

Even if I were allowed to attend this club for future "Slays," I wouldn't be seeing this Adonis in flannel.

A few patrons came in, and a couple sat on a sofa facing the fire. The club should start any moment. I'd better forget about Grant Calhoun—and about joining the club.

"Apparently, I'm just like you: not in Twelve Slays." I tugged at the hem of my cat sweater. Darn cat sweater. No wonder Mr. Everybody's Type felt nothing while I was all plugged-in-Christmas-lights. "I guess I'll come back next week—after reading the book."

"Um ..." He looked over at Freya, who was happily passing out mugs to people who obviously *had* read the Agatha Christie novel.

"Um, what?" I asked.

"If you're not admitted to Freya's club, you're not admitted to the club, period."

What? My throat constricted. "I can't come back?"

His grimace was my answer—and it gibed with what Danica had claimed.

"Seriously?" That was merciless. "No second chances?" I spluttered, my heart accelerating into criminal-speeding range. "But—"

But I just *had* to be a member of Twelve Slays of Christmas! It was the only weekly book club on Professor Higgins's *Approved Public*

Book Club List within a three-hour radius of my house. The rest met monthly—or were discussing Russian literature. I ask you! How could Russian lit meet weekly? *Anna Karenina* or *War and Peace* in a week's time? Plus, I got hopelessly lost trying to keep track of all the characters' names and nicknames. How could Sasha and Alexi and Alexander and Shuha and Shurik and so on all be the same person?

Normally, I would have said *anything* was better than crime fiction, but not Russian Literature and Latte. Although, that might be my last resort. *Please, please, please, don't make me remember Alexi is Shuha!*

"I really need to be in this group." I pleaded with Grant, as if he were the one making the decision. As if he had power to help me. "Is there anything I can do to change her mind?" We stood near the coat rack by the door, and all the group members were settling into the chairs near the fire.

"Why do you even care? In a book club, other people choose the reading material. Can't you choose your own books?" Grant held up his tome. "Life's too short to read books for pleasure that don't give you pleasure. Don't tell me you only read by assignment."

Unfortunately, when seeking a degree in literature while working full time, that held true.

"Oh, brother." He must have read the truth in my face. "What was the last book you actually *chose* for yourself?"

"A Yardley Gregson sci-fi. You've probably never heard of him." I would've flown through any of Gregson's Captain Vartigan Chronicles and loved every page turn, if a book club featuring Gregson had been on Professor Higgins's approved list.

No such luck. And changing her mind would take some kind of Christmas miracle. Higgins had Scrooge written all over her.

"You're kidding." Grant peered at me through his dark-rimmed glasses, his pupils dilating. Oh, fine. I probably imagined that.

"Kidding about what?"

"About Yardley Gregson."

"I mean, it's been a while since I read the series. I'm in school, as you probably figured out. English literature majors don't get to choose their reading material—as you said. But I have the newest one on pre-order. It comes out on Christmas Eve. I'm giving it to myself, and I'll read it when I finish up some other projects. Rewarding myself."

Mr. Everybody's Type stared at me as if I'd beamed down from a starship. "I know it comes out on Christmas Eve."

"All the fans know that. It's been a full year since *Vartigan's Longest Battle*. I heard he is a new dad, and it's taking up a lot of his writing time." His happiness was his fans' agony. "Why look so dumbfounded?"

"I don't know. I just"—he gave my cat garb a once-over—"I pegged you for a witch-with-a-black-cat cozy mystery reader, not a Vartiganian. I'm not sure I believe you."

I ignored the wardrobe slight. And the weird push-back. "It's only the best sci-fi series of all time."

"Prove you've read Gregson." Grant pulled his glasses off, deftly folding them, his eyes wide.

"Why?"

Wow. What eyes they were—and who cared if I sounded like the big bad wolf pretending to be Little Red Riding Hood's grandmother when I noted them? Large and green, with flecks of gold. They were offset by his red flannel shirt. Christmas colors, like gift-wrap, but in October.

A gift to me.

It took a second, but I gathered in the wads of torn wrapping paper my attention had become.

"I don't have to prove anything. Gregson is my author crush. I met him at a book signing in Sugarplum Falls last Christmas."

"Not proof enough." He folded his arms over his chest. He was serious about the proof? Why did he care so much?

"Okay, fine, if you're being a book tyrant. In *Princess of Chylock*, I love the scene where Captain Vartigan and the Rygraff Princess are both held prisoner and they have to work together to get out—only to be met by that alien guard with—"

"—with the ten-headed snake." He completed the sentence with me, nodding. "You really are a fan." His eyes narrowed. "Any other sci-fi authors?"

I rattled off a few of the classics—Edgar Rice Burroughs, Jules Verne, Isaac Asimov. "But I read tons of books."

"Just not *Sparkling Cyanide*." Mirth danced in his Christmassy eyes.

"I don't read crime fiction."

"Then why so desperate to join Twelve Slays of Christmas?"

"It's complicated." Nobody should be subjected to my tale of academic woe, let alone someone I'd just met. I pivoted back to my favorite topic. "Have you read Gregson's earlier series, before Captain Vartigan? The one set on *The Endeavor*?"

"You mean the most powerful intergalactic battleship of all time?"

That was the one, and it set off a full five-minute frenzy discussion of favorite scenes in that series, and two other series by Yardley Gregson.

Grant looked at me like I'd beamed down from *The Endeavor*. "I never would've dreamed I'd meet a fellow freak-fan in the Hot Chocolate Shop in Wilder River."

"Well, I'm not actually living here. I'm in town for a job." One Bitsy had told me to button my lip about. Gloss always insisted on secrecy before launching an ad campaign. They hated copycats.

"I thought you said you were in school."

"It's a freelance thing on the side." Sort of. I had a short-term contract with them, and Bitsy was hoping to make it bigger.

"Gotcha."

"Can you give me a primer on Wilder River? I heard from … someone—Danica, maybe?—that the river is special. Or its headwaters spring? Used to be a health destination, back in the day?"

The clock struck seven, and Grant didn't get a chance to answer that.

"Welcome, everyone." Freya planted herself in front of the fire, and shot glances between Grant and me. "Twelve Slays of Christmas discussion starts now."

The other patrons—there were five or six—clapped. Freya shooed us out of the seating area with a sweeping glance.

Grant nodded his head toward the other side of the room, and I followed him. We sat at the bar.

"Dark chocolate or milk chocolate?"

"Both?" I said. "I'm happy with all the chocolate."

He ordered me a mug of hot chocolate with orange extract add-in. A second later, I was sipping like a queen. "This is the perfect blend of bitterness and sweetness."

"And the orange?"

"Elevates it." I took another sip, the goodness warming me through. Finally! After being so cold all day. "Thank you. But since I'm not in the group, I should have left."

"Well, I had an ulterior motive." He looked both ways. "I needed more time to find out what else you've read."

I could talk books all day long. It was part of the reason I wanted to finish my master's degree. Not the biggest reason, but a good one.

We talked fantasy, Tolkien and Sanderson, plus a few others. He'd read those, plus some others that I took notes of. When I was done with school, I'd check them out.

As we talked and sipped our beverages, swirls of steam, citrusy and chocolaty, filled my senses. Not as much as Grant's enthusiasm for books, but also delicious.

"Read any other genres?" I asked. *Please don't launch into Russian lit.*

"I like pretty much everything." He named a few Greek classics and described them so passionately that it sounded like I'd need to check them out. "It might be unusual, but I really like Victorian authors."

"Like Dickens, you mean?"

"Yes, and Anthony Trollope. And Elizabeth Gaskell." He launched into a passionate verbal essay about the moral lessons in 1870s literature, plus how much an abundance of detail in writing wasn't always a bad thing. "It really draws me into the setting. You can't over-describe the experience of the fox hunt, I say."

Danica was not wrong. Irresistible. His vibe enveloped me. *You had me at "detailed description of riding to hounds."*

Grant Calhoun was so my type. And not just because of his broad shoulders and soulful eyes and intensely hot hot-nerd vibe.

"How have you read all this stuff? Were you an English major?" That would've made two of us.

"Chemistry," he said in a sultry voice that I probably only imagined.

Chemistry was right. It swirled around in the air like the chocolate essence of the Hot Chocolate Shop.

I had to leave. Right now. Before I forgot all the vital responsibilities of my life—including finding a book club that would accept me.

"Thanks for the chat." I drained the mug, dug around in my purse with a nod, and left some cash on the table. He handed it back to me, and I placed it in my purse. "Danica was right when she told me I'd be glad I met you." Wow. I just blabbed. I sounded desperate. And I was never desperate.

"Bye!" I dashed toward the door before I could say anything else, or do anything unwise, like offer him my number and beg him to call me. Tonight. Keep the chat going.

I placed my hand on the doorknob to leave, when Freya raised her voice.

"Twelve Slays of Christmas almost had a new member tonight." Freya cleared her throat. "Isn't that right, Roxanna Reid?"

I stopped cold. Was she changing her mind? Had she heard Grant's and my book discussion and decided I wasn't a flake about reading after all? "I'm going to really miss out," I said over my shoulder. *Please, let me in!*

Freya stepped toward me. "Since it was her first week in the club, and she hadn't been briefed on the normally hard-and-fast rules of our group, I'm considering offering her a chance to stay."

I swung around. If my hair had been free from the cat beanie, it would have swung in a perfect, photogenic arc that sweet old Domingo would've loved.

"Really?" I squeaked in a voice matching the cats I wore. "That would mean the world to me." Elation surged through me. A round of hot chocolate with any add-in for everyone in Wilder River! "Are you giving me a second chance?" Again with the desperation, the begging tone I tried so hard never to reveal.

Freya's stern tone resumed. "My offer is good on one condition." Her head swiveled, hawk-like, and she pinned her gaze on Grant. "Roxanna Reid, you can join Twelve Slays of Christmas *if* you read all the other books before arriving at the book club discussion."

"Of course." Obviously!

Freya wasn't through. "*And* if Grant Calhoun joins."

Read *The Hot Chocolate Shop* next and discover Roxanna's secret that unwittingly makes her Grant's biggest enemy—even if they're falling in love.

Bonus Recipe from the Griffith Family: Strawberry Dessert

This recipe that Jeremy makes is a family favorite at all the Griffith parties, brought by super dessert-maker, Julie.

6 oz strawberry jell-o
2 c boiling water
2.5 c pretzels (crush into medium-fine chunks)
¼ c sugar
½ c butter
8 oz cream cheese (room temp)
½ c sugar
8 oz Cool Whip
1 lb strawberries, sliced

Mix jell-o powder and water, set aside to cool to room temperature. In a saucepan over medium heat, melt butter and ¼ cup sugar. Stir. Mix in crushed pretzels. Pour mixture into 9x13 pan, press to level. Bake 10 min at 350*. Cool to room temperature. Beat cream cheese and ½ c sugar with hand mixer to fluffy. Fold in thawed Cool Whip well. Spread over cooled pretzel crust. Spread to edges to create tight seal. Refrigerate 30 min. Stir strawberries into room-temp jell-o liquid. Pour evenly over cream cheese layer. Refrigerate 2 hours or until set. Cut and serve. Pretend it's a salad.

Christmas House Romance Series

The Christmas Cookie House
The Sleigh Bells Chalet
The Holiday Hunting Lodge
The Peppermint Drop Inn
The Candy Cane Cottage
The Hot Chocolate Shop
Starlight Haven
The Candlelight Chapel
The Mistletoe Lift
Yuletide Manor

All books this series of clean Christmas romances celebrate family, tradition, Christmas, belief, and love. They are all standalone romances, but they do connect in the small town world and can be best enjoyed in a "loop." Book 1 leads to book 2, and so on, and at the end, book 10 loops back to book 1, with recurring characters. In other words, a reader can start with any book, read the subsequent book, and then complete the loop.

About the Author

Jennifer Griffith is the *USA Today* bestselling author of over fifty novels and novellas. Two of her novels have received the Swoony Award for best secular romance novel of the year. She lives in Arizona with her husband, who is a judge and her muse. They are the parents of five brilliant children.

Connect with Jennifer at authorjennifergriffith.com, where you can sign up for her newsletter to receive exclusive content and notices of new releases.

Made in the USA
Middletown, DE
09 December 2024

66512195R00115